ESCAPING SARA

JEANNA M. MARESCALCHI

To my Aunt Lorraine (Boisvert) and my Aunt Shirley (Marescalchi) for always seeing the good in me, even when I can't. You both allow me to express my thoughts and feelings without judgement. You accept me for who I am and are always there to lend an ear. Your kind words and encouragement are appreciated more than you could ever know and because of each of you, I will continue writing!

TABLE OF CONTENTS

ACKNOWLEDGEMENTS

I would like to thank YOU, my readers, for your continued support and consistent feedback. Without your honest reviews, opinions, and constructive criticism, I would not be able to successfully do what I love to do!

FROM THE AUTHOR

As you read this fictional story, I hope you find it suspenseful and intriguing. My goal is to entertain you and capture your attention as you attempt to predict the unpredictable ending.

My name is Sara Frost. I am a waitress and mother of twin girls, Kya, and Kailey. My daughters have never met their father because he died in a car accident when I was three months pregnant. I had never met his family but did briefly attend his funeral from a distance at the cemetery. I had not made myself known to anyone that day nor have I ever tried to contact his family since. I kept my pregnancy a secret and to this day, I continue to keep that secret to myself, but I always knew some day that secret would eventually come out. I had always struggled growing up. I wish I could erase most of my childhood from my mind. My father left my mother and I when I was just five years old and took my older brother, Ben, with him. I have never seen or heard from either one of them since that day and soon after they left, my mother would have different men come and go in her life. She would drink every day from morning 'til night and every weekend she would have parties at the house which always involved cocaine. Of course, at five years old, I had thought it was flour on the coffee table. Eventually, my mother died from an overdose. I was eleven. After she passed, I went to live with my grandmother but I was always left alone at night so she could go play bingo. She was a bit of a drinker as well, so I rarely made it to school on time. Other than my grandmother, I had no family, at least not of which I was aware. My grandmother eventually passed away and I was forced to live on my own later in my teens. I began waitressing at various pubs while staying with anyone who allowed me to sleep on their couch. This went on for years until I was finally able to save enough money to get my own place, which was a small apartment building in the center of town and that is where I eventually met Jonathan. We had dated for quite a while before he asked me to marry him. I, of course, said yes. I loved him with all my heart, and I couldn't wait to be his wife. We were so happy together, but he hadn't spoken with anyone in his family for quite some time therefore, I did not know much about them, and they did not know I even existed. The day of the accident was also the day I had found out I was pregnant. I hadn't told him. I had spoken with him over the phone earlier that day but wanted to wait to tell him in person as I had a special idea to surprise him. I knew he would have been excited as we had always talked about having kids though we did plan to have them after we were married.

A few years after my children were born, I met Derek. He was the head cook at the pub I used to work at. In fact, he was the one who interviewed and hired me for the waitressing position. I hadn't worked for a while since I didn't have anybody to watch my kids and I couldn't afford daycare. I was still living off the money from my grandmother's life insurance but that was running out quickly.

When Derek and I started dating, after a one-night stand, he seemed like such a nice guy, and he accepted my children as part of the package. We moved in with him to an apartment just outside of town. He took care of me and my girls financially and I was able to go back to waitressing at the pub I had worked at before and a neighbor, her name was Nancy, had volunteered to babysit the girls while I was at work. Nancy and I had become friends though at times, I felt a little bit uneasy leaving the kids with her because she would often treat the girls as if they were hers but when I would mention it to her, she would just tell me it is because she liked them and didn't have kids of her own. Derek always told me I was overreacting whenever I brought it up to him.

Derek and I were working at the pub together, but we had different shifts every other week. It didn't take long before things drastically changed. Derek would not come home from work until the early morning hours and the pub closed at midnight, so I knew he wasn't working until 3am. He would also come home drunk or smelling like marijuana. Then he started calling out from work and just sitting in the apartment, drinking, and smoking pot all day and night. He would get aggressive with me whenever I questioned him about work or asked him to clean up his empty beer cans and whisky bottles. He did hit me and push me around every now and then. He never laid his hands on the girls, but he would scare them often. I wanted so much to leave him, but I did not know how or where I was going to go.

 Then one evening, I came home a little late from work. I had worked a double shift. Nancy had watched the girls during my first shift but then Derek was home with them during the second. When I walked in, the living room was a mess as usual. The girls were asleep in their room and Derek was out on the back deck talking to someone on his phone. When he noticed I was home, he quickly ended his conversation. We talked for a few minutes then he went to take a shower before heading to bed. While he was in the shower, I heard his phone go off. He had left it on his dresser. It was a text message, so I opened it. It was from Nancy. It read:

 IT'S TIME. I WILL GRAB THE KIDS IN THE MORNING AND MEET YOU WHERE WE DISCUSSED. STICK WITH THE PLAN AND THE GIRLS WILL FINALLY BE WHERE THEY BELONG!

 After reading that text, I knew something was going on though I wasn't sure exactly what. I assumed Nancy and Derek were having an affair, but I didn't even bother to question Derek. I just wanted to get myself and my girls out of the house. So, I waited until the middle of the night when Derek was sleeping, or should I say passed out then I woke up Kya and Kailey and the three of us, without much packed other than a few duffle bags, and a wad of cash I had been saving from my work tips I had hidden under my mattress, we quietly snuck out of the apartment, started up the car and went on our way to wherever we were going.

I had been driving for hours. I had already crossed three state lines. The girls had fallen asleep in the back seat but not before asking many questions about why we were leaving and where we were going. At the time, I really couldn't give them any answers. Of course, they were upset but they trusted me, and they knew I would always keep them safe. I was lucky enough to find a gas station when needed to fill my tank here and there since there was nothing else around except for acres of farmland but I didn't want to wake the girls and I was not going to leave them alone in the car for even a minute so I could not go in to grab any snacks at each stop though I knew they would be hungry when they woke up.

The sun was rising, and I was still driving, hoping to find a place to stop and feed the girls. I had crossed over into yet another state. There was a small sign that read "Welcome to Bandana, Kentucky, Population 200." I thought to myself, this would be a good place to start over. Then, ahead on the right side of the road, I noticed a big flashing sign that read "Dot's Diner." I pulled into the dirt lot, parked the car, and woke the girls. "Kya, Kailey" as I shook them both a little, "Wake up girls, we're going to get some breakfast." They both jumped up. Kailey yelled, "Yay! I'm starving!" and Kya laughed. The girls were ready to get out of the car, but I knew I needed to talk to them first. "Hey, not so fast," I said calmly. "Mommy needs to talk to you both," I cleared my throat, "when we go into this diner, we cannot say anything about our road trip." The girls looked at me with confusion. I continued, "and I cannot call you by your real names." Kya asked with a sad tone, "But why Mommy? I like my name." I put my head down for a minute. "I know you do honey and so do I but for now, we will call you Mia and your sister will be Mandy." Kailey said with a smile, "Oh, I like the name Mandy." Then they both asked, "What are you going to call yourself, Mommy?" I responded rather quickly, "Julie...I am going to call myself Julie," I always did like that name, and I had a close childhood friend named Julie, "and our last name will be Banks," I added.

  As we walked into the diner, I couldn't help but feel as if everyone were staring at the three of us. I felt extremely uncomfortable standing in the doorway until an older woman wearing a waitress uniform with beautiful blonde hair up in a high bun approached us. She looked like someone from back in the fifties though the diner also had a fifties-style décor. "Y'all can sit anywhere you'd like." She said with a heavy southern accent. So, the girls and I chose a booth in the back of the diner. Shortly after *we sat down, the same woman came over. "Well, aren't you two little girls just as cute as pie." Kya smiled at her and started to say, "Thank you, my name is Ky- "I had to interrupt quickly. "That's Mia and this is Mandy." "I've never seen y'all in here before, are you new in town?" asked the waitress. I answered, "Um, no, we're just passing through." She then asked, "Where y'all headin'?" I looked at the girls then replied. "Uh, not sure yet, just taking a little trip." The woman paused for a moment before asking me, "Sweetie, what's your name?" "It's Julie," I responded, "Julie Banks." "Well, Julie, I hope you're not lost darlin'." Just then Kailey, well, Mandy, said "Mommy, we don't know where we're going so doesn't that mean we're lost?" The woman didn't say anything for a couple of minutes and neither did I. Then she said as she looked at me, "Honey, my name is Dottie. I own this little slice of heaven here. If there is anything you need, you just let me know." I said thank you and we ordered our lunch. The girls both ordered pancakes and I ordered the breakfast special which was a western omelet. I had never been to a real diner before, so I was looking forward to a nice home cooked meal. When Dottie delivered our food to the table, she said in her sweet voice, "Breakfast is on me today." I quickly told her, "You don't need to do that for us." She then said, "I know I don't, but I want to. Like I said, I own this place. Y'all enjoy!"*

When we were finished eating, the girls and I used the restroom, went to thank Dottie again for breakfast then headed out to get back on our way to wherever we were going. It was late in the afternoon, and we hadn't had anything to eat since breakfast, but I couldn't find another place to stop and get something to eat other than a gas station. So, the three of us went in to grab some snacks and drinks to tie us over until we could find somewhere to have dinner. It was evening and I had been driving for miles and getting hungry and tired. The girls were sleeping, both snuggling with their favorite stuffed animals. Kailey, with her puppy and Kya with her bunny. Looking back at the two of them, I realized I needed to find a place to stay at least for the night so they could sleep more comfortably. After driving for another hour or so, I decided to turn around and head back to the diner.

When I arrived back there, I noticed the CLOSED sign on the door but could see Dottie through the window, cleaning tables. I woke the girls and the three of us walked up to the door and knocked softly. I heard Dottie yell, "Sorry, we're closed, come back tomorrow!" As we were turning away, she came to the door. She opened it and said, "Hey y'all, I didn't know it was you. How can I help you?" I hesitated briefly before responding. "Um, do you know of a hotel close by?" Dottie replied, "Oh no sugar, there ain't a hotel or even a motel for miles from here." I *put my head down and as the kids were telling me how hungry and tired they were, Dottie invited us in. "Let me make y'all something for dinner." The three of us sat at the counter while Dottie went out back to the kitchen to cook us something to eat. It didn't take too long for her to come back out carrying three plates of meatloaf dinners, which ironically happened to be the girls' favorite meal. As they were indulging in their food, Dottie told me to sit down with her a couple of booths away so she and I could talk. "I didn't want to chat in front of the kids," she said, "It's Julie, right?" "Yes," I said. "Honey, I don't know what's going on with you, but I happen to know of a small cottage just down the road a bit. You and the girls can stay there if you'd like." "Oh," I said, "do you know who owns it?" I asked. "Well, as a matter of fact I do," she smiled, "it is on my property a few hundred feet away from my home." I breathed a sigh of relief, "Um, I do want my girls to get a good night sleep tonight." I gave her a smile and she said, "Well, then, let me close up everything here and we shall be on our way.*

When we arrived at the cottage, which was just down the road as she said, the girls got excited. It was small but it was lovely. It was dark but right away, we noticed the window boxes with beautiful bright colored flowers. The cottage was painted a dark barn red color with bright white trim. It had a quaint little front porch with two wooden rocking chairs. Dottie's house was just a short distance away. The pebbled driveway connected both properties. Once we parked, we unloaded our bags from the trunk. Dottie walked over with the keys to the cottage and was carrying a mound of fresh towels, bed sheets, blankets, and pillows. "Here y'all are!" she said as we entered. The girls immediately climbed up the ladder to the loft. "Mommy, can we sleep up here tonight?" they both asked with a big smile. "Yes," I responded, "of course you can but I think you better unpack, brush your teeth, and get ready for bed. It's been a long day and you need to rest." Just then, Dottie said, "Yea, that's a great idea! Your mommy and I will be right outside on the porch." I looked around a minute and then had to ask, "Um, Dottie, there isn't a back door in here, is there?" She replied quickly, "Oh no Honey, just the front door," and she continued to say in a reassuring way, "you and your girls are safe here."

Once the girls were settled, I went out to meet Dottie on the porch. She made hot tea for us to drink. She started with some small talk, not much about anything but I knew she was curious as to what we were doing there. As sweet and generous as she was, I was still nervous and scared to tell her anything. I didn't know this woman and I didn't know if I could trust her. Trusting people, well, the wrong people, was what got me to this point.

After about twenty minutes of conversation about the diner, Dottie finally asked, "Darling, are you running from something or someone?" I cleared my throat and sighed before answering her. "I'm just trying to keep my daughters safe." "Well," she said as she put her hand over mine, "I'm not one to pry or get into other people's business but I don't want any trouble either." She removed her hand and took a sip of her tea. "I've owned the diner since my grandma, Dot, passed away many years ago and I know a lot of people in this small town, though there ain't many people here. This ain't no place to keep secrets so if there's something I should know, you can tell me and maybe I can help." "We're going to be fine," I replied, "I've done what I needed to do." At that moment, our conversation ended and as we were saying goodnight to one another, I said to Dottie, "Thank you again for letting us stay here tonight. We will be out in the morning." She said in a caring way, "Sugar, why don't you and your girls stay until you get all your ducks in a row, however long that takes. Gosh, I haven't had anyone stay in this cottage since my niece got kicked out of her apartment but that's a story for another night." "Are you sure?" I asked and she answered, "Why yes, I'm sure, it's no bother! Besides, I'd love the company. It can get a little lonely every now and then. In case you hadn't noticed, other than my diner, there ain't much else around here but gas stations and mini marts." "Well," I said, "that's very generous of you. I will talk to the girls in the morning and ask what they think." Kailey and Kya, I mean Mandy and Mia, were both sound asleep up in the loft. I laid in bed for most of the night, just staring up at the ceiling, wondering what to do next. It made sense to me to take Dottie up on her offer and I could see the girls and I staying there, at least for the rest of the summer. It would allow me more time to figure out a plan before they needed to go back to school.

The sun came up and I had not slept much at all. As the girls were climbing down the ladder, Kya asked, "Mommy, we don't have to leave here today, do we?" I put my arms around each of them and replied, "No. No girls. We don't have to leave today. In fact, Dottie said we can stay here for as long as we want." Both girls were jumping up and down and yelling "Yay!" Then, there was a knock on the door. I quickly told the girls to get into the bathroom and lock the door. I became jumpy. I tip-toed to the door and asked before opening, "Who's there?" "Good morning Darlin,' it's just me, Dottie." I released a deep breath and opened the door. "Oh, good morning, I'm sorry, I-" She interrupted. "No need to apologize, I didn't mean to startle you. I was just coming over here to tell you it's breakfast time. I made some fresh eggs, bacon and toast for you and your girls. Why don't you make your way over to my house before it all gets cold." "Thank you, we will be right there!" I said, then I went to get the girls. Breakfast was delicious and I had not seen the girls eat as much as they did for quite some time, other than their meatloaf dinners the night before.

After breakfast, Dottie gave the girls and I a tour around her rather large home. It had four bedrooms and two bathrooms with a finished attic and basement. The girls were in awe as was I. I had never been in such a big house before. Though it was quite outdated, it still had a lot of charm to it. But there was one room Dottie didn't show us and when the girls asked her what that room was for, Dottie just told them, "Oh, it's filled with clutter, nothin' to see in there." So, I told the girls to just move along.

After the tour, we went back into the kitchen, and I helped Dottie clean the dishes. The girls were in the den watching tv. We were chatting a bit when suddenly, the doorbell rang. It startled me and I dropped the dish I was drying, and it smashed on the floor. "Honey, it's okay," said Dottie, "I'll pick that all up after I see who is at the door." I ran int the den and grabbed the girls and ran to the upstairs bathroom. I knew I frightened them, but I was frightened, too. I could hear Dottie talking with someone down in the kitchen. It was a man's voice, and I was even more frightened. I thought to myself, what if it was Derek? Or the police? Or someone else looking for me? Then Dottie came upstairs and tapped on the bathroom door. She said in a soft voice, "Honey, it's me. Everything's all right. I want you to come down and meet my nephew. Don't worry, it's fine." She went back downstairs but before the girls and I left the bathroom, I reminded them to call themselves by their new names.

When we walked into the kitchen, there was a man, a very handsome man, with a strong build, wearing a tight plaid shirt and blue jeans. He had a thin beard and wore a cowboy hat and boots. He was sweeping up the mess I had made. He looked at me and said, "I guess you're the one who broke the dish, huh?" I smirked at him, "Yes, it was an accident." He replied, "No worries, I wasn't implying you did it on purpose. I just hope you didn't cut yourself." "No, I'm fine," I said. Just then, Dottie said, "Julie, this is my nephew, Blake Tobin. He comes by to visit his old aunt occasionally and helps with the landscaping when it gets overgrown." She then turned to Blake and said, "Blake, this is Julie, and these precious little angels are her girls...what are their names again?" I answered quickly before the girls did just in case they forgot. "Oh, this is Mandy," I said, pointing to Kailey, "and this is Mia," as I pointed to Kya. It was even confusing for me; I couldn't imagine how hard it was for the girls to keep their names straight. Blake had put his hand out to shake mine as he said, "Well, it's nice to meet you, Julie," and as he looked over at the girls, he said, "and it's nice to meet the two of you. He then said as he put his arm around his aunt, "Don't let my aunt fool you, I come by here often to see her and help her whenever I can. She's been a like mother to me since I lost my mom years ago." "Well," replied Dottie, "I promised my sister I would take care of you." He then gave her a kiss on her cheek. It was obvious they had a close relationship though Dottie hadn't mentioned him in our earlier conversations but then again, I hadn't mentioned much about my family, or lack of one, either. Blake seemed friendly enough, but I knew nothing about him.

After a few minutes of small talk, Blake offered to take the girls and I for a walk around the property. I wasn't too sure of the idea at first but then Dottie assured me that it would be okay, and she whispered in my ear telling me I could trust him. She also told us there were many interesting things to see out in the back woods and that the girls would enjoy it. So, the four of us went out on our way.

 As we were walking, Blake was telling the girls stories about the property and the three of them were hunting for special-colored rocks and looking for different types of wildflowers. They were having fun and they both seemed to really like Blake. As for him and me, there wasn't much said between the two us. I was rather quiet, but I was also more concerned with Kya and Kailey. We had been out in the woods for about an hour when we came up to a beautiful clear-blue stream surrounded by flowers in all sorts of colors. Blake then assisted the girls and I, one by one, up to the top of an enormous rock. The four of us stood there and looked all around at the picturesque scenery. It was very peaceful and seemed as though we were looking at a painting. Everything was perfect. Out of the corner of my eye, I could see Blake staring at me with a little smile. I turned to him and smiled back. We finished our walk and started to head back to the house.

 When we arrived, the girls were running around the humongous yard, laughing, and chasing each other. I was so happy to see them happy. Then, Blake asked what I did not want him to ask, "Hey Julie, do you think I could take you out for dinner tonight?" I didn't say anything then he continued, "I know a nice little tavern about thirty miles from here, with good food and great drinks. They even have live music." I took a moment before answering him. "I don't want to be that far from the girls," then I did what I really didn't want to do and said, "I'm sorry but I can't...girls, come on, we need to get back to the cottage," and the three of us abruptly left.

 The next afternoon, I was sitting out on the porch reading a book when suddenly, Blake drove up the driveway. He got out of his truck and started walking towards me. I put my book down and met him halfway. We both said, "I'm sorry" at the same time, then he said, "I didn't mean to make you uncomfortable when I asked you to go out last night." I gave him a little smile and said, "I just have a lot going on right now and I need time to clear my head." He nodded and replied, "I understand." He paused a minute then said, "I need to see my aunt about something. Let's talk again soon." I responded, "I 'd like that."

CHAPTER

FOUR

For the next several weeks, I didn't see much of Blake. He would only stop by Dottie's once in a while to help her with yard work. He would give me a quick wave when I was out on the porch but that was all. I kind of missed him and the girls would ask every now and then where he was.

It was nearing the end of summer and I knew it was time to get the girls enrolled in school. Dottie took us to the closest school, Colton Public, which was quite a distance away, but she said a bus would pick up the girls at the end of the driveway in the mornings and drop them off in the afternoons. On the first day of school, Mandy and Mia were both excited and a little nervous but they got off the bus that afternoon with big smiles and said they had a fun day and met lots of new friends. I was so relieved and happy our new life seemed to be going well for them. I, on the other hand, had wished things were going better for me. I missed Blake and wanted so much to contact him, but I also didn't want to rush into anything. About a month passed and I still hadn't talked to him. I would go to work at the diner every day hoping to see him then finally one day, he walked in. I couldn't help but smile at him and he smiled back then came over to the counter where I was standing. "Hey Julie," he said, "How have you been?" I answered, "I've been okay." "Dottie told me your girls started Colton Public," he continued, "I'm glad they seem to be settling in alright." "Yes," I replied, "they seem to be adjusting well." After some small talk about the kids and work, Blake then asked, "Can we pick up where we left off? I know it's been a while, but I would love to get to know you better and I promise I won't pressure you." I smiled at him and quickly responded, "That would be great!"

A few evenings later, Blake and I went to the tavern he mentioned before. Dottie offered to have the girls stay at her house and I was finally comfortable enough to leave them, at least for a little while. When we walked into the tavern, I felt awkward as I wasn't all dolled up in a cowgirl getup like the other women. It looked like a country saloon, but it was a lot of fun! I met some friends of Blake's and some of Dottie's as well. I even saw some of the customers I serve at the diner. I actually felt as if I belonged there. Blake and I danced and drank and danced some more and drank some more. After a few hours and much too much to drink, I asked Blake to take me home.

When we arrived back at the cottage, Blake walked me to the front door. Dottie was inside and had put the girls to bed. We looked at each other for what seemed like a long time then he leaned over to kiss me. I quickly backed away without saying a word but after a few seconds, I found myself grabbing him by his neck and kissing him. I think he was just as shocked as I was. What seemed like an exceptionally long kiss had ended and we both smiled at one another and chuckled a bit. Then, I asked him if he wanted to come in for a nightcap. To my surprise, he did not. He said it was because he didn't want things to go too fast between us. I understood and it was probably for the best since I had consumed way too much alcohol.

The next morning as the girls were waiting at the end of the driveway for the school bus, I was sitting on the porch and Blake pulled in. He stopped to talk to the girls before parking his truck. When he came out of his truck, I noticed he was holding a bouquet of flowers. He then walked up to me. "These are for you, Julie. I had a nice time with you last night and I would like to have more nights like that with you," he said as he handed me the flowers. "Wow!" I replied, "these are beautiful and yes, I enjoyed myself, too!" I could hear the girls giggling and see them whispering to each other then the bus showed up. "Have a great day, girls!" I yelled at them from the porch. Blake gave them a big wave and they both yelled, "Bye Blake, see you when we get home from school!" That is the moment I realized the girls really liked him and

I knew being in a relationship with him would be okay with them.

After the bus drove away, Blake looked at me and asked, "So, what should we do today?" I smiled at him and responded, "Anything you want." "Okay then, let's get in the truck and just go to wherever we end up." "Great!" I said, then I thought to myself, this is how I got here in the first place. We were driving for about a half an hour before he pulled down a dirt road off the main street. Then we drove another ten minutes or so and ahead there was a log cabin with a farmer's porch wrapped around it, surrounded by pine trees. He pulled up and said, "Here we are!" "Who lives here?" I asked. "I do. I built this place five years ago," he said, "I want to show you inside and you won't believe the view from the back deck." As we walked into the cabin, I could smell fresh roses then I saw a large bouquet of them on the mantel of the fireplace. He noticed that I was staring at them and said as he put his arm around me, "Those are for you." I was incredibly surprised he had more flowers for me. He then said, "Come on, I want to show you around."

He gave me the tour of the cabin which was well designed and had a masculine décor with a bit of a female touch. It had two bedrooms, one and a half bathrooms, a small eat-in kitchen, and a fairly big living room. In his bedroom, there was a photo on the nightstand of Blake and a woman holding a young boy. I pretended I didn't see it and he quickly moved on to show me the rest of the cabin. Then he opened the French doors leading to the back deck. "Close your eyes," he said as he walked me out, "now open them." I couldn't believe what I was looking at. It was beautiful. "Those are the Appalachian Mountains," he said and asked, "What do you think?" I had a tear in my eye as I answered him, "I think I could live here for the rest of my life." He leaned over and kissed me. "Let's go back inside and I'll cook brunch for us."

 After brunch, which was delicious, we took our mimosas out to the back deck. Not much was spoken at first, we were both just taking in the view. Then I had to ask Blake, since I was curious, "Who are the woman and child in the photo on your nightstand?" He paused a moment, then said in a quiet voice, "They were my wife and son." I took a minute before asking, "What do you mean were?" He cleared his throat and put down his drink. "Jolene, my wife, died three years ago, from breast cancer. When she was diagnosed at stage four, she said she always wanted to live in a log cabin," he cleared his throat again and continued, "I built her this so she could live the remaining time she had left here." I held his hand then asked, "and your son?" He quickly stood up and said, "He died, too, but I can't talk about that right now." And he went back into the cabin.

After a few minutes, I walked into the kitchen to find Blake bent over the sink with his head down. I came up behind him and said, "Blake, I am sorry, I shouldn't have asked about the photo." He turned around and replied, "It's okay, I'm just not ready to talk about it." I said, "And you don't have to." He then put his arms around me, "Let's go for a walk." But instead, we started kissing, then one thing led to another and within minutes, we were tearing off each other's clothes. He picked me up and carried me to his bedroom and we were making love. I didn't want it to end. When we were finished, we were just lying in the bed, holding each other and Blake said to me, "He died out in the lake." I sat up. "Your son?" I asked as then I laid my head on his chest. "I took him fishing...we were in my boat when..." I lifted my head up and saw tears running down his face. "You don't have to tell me right now." "I want to...I haven't been able to talk about it with anyone before." He wiped his face with his hands and continued, "I tied the boat to the dock and went down to the cabin to grab a beer out of the frig and I heard splashes, but I thought it was Tommy throwing back all the fish we had caught so I didn't rush back out to the deck but when I did..." He paused and didn't say another word for a couple minutes then he continued, "he had fallen off the boat, but I couldn't see him." My eyes started to well up. "It was an accident, Blake, it wasn't your fault." He quickly interrupted me. "It was my fault; I should've had a life jacket on him! He was only four years old!" He then said, "I had always put a life jacket on him but this time, I forgot. I was more concerned with drinking my beer, I should have never even had him out on the lake with me. It was only a few weeks after Jolene's death, I wasn't in my right mind to even take care of my son." He then sat up on the side of the bed. I sat behind him and wrapped my arms around him. "You have to get past this. Neither your wife nor your son would want you to blame yourself like this." Blake stood up and put on his boxers. "Let's go for that walk now." Then I got up while covering myself with the bedsheet and said, "I need to get back to be there when the girls get home from school." On the drive home, Blake was quiet. We didn't talk about his wife or son, but we did hold hands for a while.

We arrived just as the school bus was pulling over to the side of the road. As we drove into the driveway, Dottie was standing there waiting for the girls to get off the bus. She looked at us and said, "Well, I see you two are gettin' along pretty well with one another." Blake replied quickly, "Auntie, don't go making a big deal out of nothing." I stood there, in disbelief to what I had just heard come out of Blake's mouth. After all, I thought we had just had the most amazing day together. I thought we had just started a relationship with each other. When the girls got off the bus, I told them to go to the cottage to empty their backpacks and start doing their homework. Before Dottie had left, I asked her, "What are you doing here Dottie, I thought you would be at the diner?" She replied, "Well, honey, I wanted to be here when the girls got home from school, just in case you weren't here on time." "Oh," I said, "thank you." Dottie walked back to her house, and I started walking to the cottage. Blake then asked, "Where are you going?" I quickly responded, "I need to see my girls. Besides, I don't want any of this to be a big deal!" and I started walking away. He gently grabbed my arm, "Julie, I didn't mean to imply what we have here is nothing. It's just that I don't really want my aunt to know much right now. She has been pressuring me for quite a while since Jolene's passing to get, as she says, back on the horse again. I don't want to feel rushed by her." He then held my hand and continued, "I love what we've started, and I want to continue being with you every chance I get." I smiled at him and replied, "Me, too," I gave him a kiss on his cheek, "your aunt just wants you to be happy...and I want to be that person who can make you happy." We kissed each other goodbye and made plans to see each other the next evening.

It was the next day, and I was having Blake over for dinner with the girls and me. They were excited to have him coming over. I had spent the day preparing and simmering a pasta sauce I had made from scratch using fresh tomatoes from Dottie's Garden.

The day seemed to go by fast and before I knew it, Blake was knocking on the door. When I opened it, he leaned over and kissed me then he handed me a bottle of wine. He had two gift bags with him and said, "I hope you don't mind, but I got each of the girls a little something." "Oh, it's fine. I'm sure they will love it!" As he walked in, I called the girls to come down from the loft. They opened their bags which had a stuffed teddy bear in each. They both gave Blake hugs. I was happy to see them so happy.

Dinner was great! Blake helped me with the dishes while the girls got ready for bed. When they were asleep, Blake and I sat out on the porch to finish off the bottle of wine. It didn't take long before we were making love in my bed, and he ended up spending the night.

The next morning was Saturday, so the girls slept in. When I woke up, I rolled over to see that Blake was not there then I noticed a note on the nightstand. It read:

I HAD TO LEAVE EARLY AND DIDN'T WANT TO WAKE YOU. I WILL CALL YOU LATER. I HAD FUN LAST NIGHT.

I smiled, placed the note back on the nightstand and went into the kitchen to get breakfast for the girls but then I noticed I didn't have enough milk for their cereal, so I woke the girls up, told them I was running next door and to lock the door behind me. I knocked on Dottie's door, but she didn't come to the door. Her car was in the driveway, so I knocked again then realized the door was unlocked. As I entered, I yelled out her name, but she didn't answer. I walked past the staircase and could faintly hear her talking to someone from upstairs so as I began walking up the stairs, I yelled her name again. She came running to the top of the stairs. "Oh, Julie, I didn't hear you come in." I apologized to her, "I'm sorry, I didn't mean to just walk in, but your door was unlocked, and I yelled your name a couple of times." "Oh," she said, "that's fine, you're welcome to walk in anytime." As she walked down the stairs, I told her I was out of milk and asked if I could have some for the girls' cereal. She told me to follow her into the kitchen and she would get me some. When we were in the kitchen, she asked, "Can I get you a cup of coffee?" I replied, "Yes, I'd loved one." We got to talking about Blake, of course, and she was telling me about some funny stories from when he was kid. After a little while, I needed to use the bathroom so I asked if I could, but she told me to use the one upstairs because there was a plumbing issue with the one downstairs.

 As I was on my way to the bathroom, I walked by the room Dottie hadn't shown us and said was filled with clutter. I knew I should have just headed straight to the bathroom, but instead, I stopped in front of that room and turned the handle of the door. It wasn't locked so I opened it. When I walked in, I was completely surprised. It was not filled with clutter at all, in fact, it was quite the opposite. It was a bedroom, decorated for a child. Of course, it was outdated but still adorable. It was clean and bright. The bed was fully made and had dolls and teddy bears perfectly placed on top of the bedspread. The walls were covered in butterfly printed wallpaper. There was a beautiful wooden vanity with a velvet covered seat. A homemade doll house and an antique looking toy chest. I opened the vanity drawer and in it was a pink hairbrush. When I picked it up, I noticed strands of blonde hair wound in it. I also noticed a small pair of white slippers on the floor next to the bed then I saw a framed photo on the nightstand. I went over to it and picked it up. It was a photo of a little girl with blonde hair in ponytails and blue eyes. I could see the resemblance to Dottie.

Just then, I heard a noise and when I turned around, Dottie was standing in the doorway. I jumped and said, "Oh, Dottie, you startled me." "What are you doing in here?" she asked. She sounded upset with me. "I'm sorry, I was on my way to the bathroom and I just..." I didn't know what to say. "It's alright," she said. I then asked while I was still holding the photo, "Who is she?" Dottie sighed then walked over to the bed and sat down. I sat next to her. "That's my daughter. Her name was Annie." I replied, "She's beautiful. She looks a lot like you." Then I asked, "What happened to her?" She put her head down before answering. "She went out for a bike ride and never came home." I quietly said, "That's awful." She continued, "It was the day after her tenth birthday. I gave her the bicycle as a present and she hounded me to let her ride it on the street. Back then, it was just a dirt road, and no one ever traveled on it unless they lived here or were lost..." She paused a moment, "I went out looking for her because it was time for supper but..." I saw a tear running down Dottie's cheek. "You don't have to talk about this if you don't want to." She replied, "I want to. It was a long time ago." "Was she abducted?" I asked. "That's what everyone suspected since they found her bicycle on the side of the road about a half mile away...but the police never had any leads." She took a deep breath. "I still have her bike, it's in the shed outback...I come in here and talk to her once in a while. I'm afraid if I get rid of her things, I might forget about her." I put my hand on her shoulder. "Dottie, she will always be with you, in your heart." "Yes," she said, "I know but if I didn't get her that bike..." I quickly said, "You can't blame yourself. It's not your fault. There are many awful people in the world." She then said, "Well, I hope they find her one day, one way or another, before I am no longer on this earth because I won't be able to rest in peace otherwise." I placed the photo back on the nightstand and gave Dottie a hug. We then walked out of the room, and I went to use the bathroom before I met her downstairs. She handed me a carton of milk and said, "Maybe that's why I gravitated to your girls so quickly. They both remind me a little of Annie, especially Mandy, that little girl is full of spunk just like my Annie was." We smiled at each other, and I left to go back next door.

 The girls and I spent the afternoon inside the cottage doing arts and crafts then outside for a bit walking around the property. I was still waiting to hear from Blake but never did. I tried calling and texting him a couple times, but his phone went straight to voicemail, and he didn't reply to any of my texts. It was getting late into the evening, so I went over to

Dottie's to ask if she had heard from him, but she said she hadn't.

 In the middle of the night, I was awakened by loud knocking on the front door and then I heard Dottie's voice. She was screaming my name. I jumped out of bed and ran to the door. When I opened it, she was frantic. "Dottie, what's wrong?" She quickly replied, "I tried calling you, but your phone is off. It's Blake!" I said in a worried tone, "My battery died, I was charging it. What about Blake?" "He's been in a car accident!" I became nervous. "What? Is he okay?" I asked. She responded, "I don't know, the hospital just contacted me and said I should get there as soon as I can." She started crying. "Well, we'll all go," I said, "let me get the girls up and we'll go!" Dottie said she would wait in her car for us, but I told her I would drive. The closest hospital was forty-five minutes away.

 When we arrived at the hospital, we all ran into the emergency entrance. I went right over to the nurse's station while Dottie stayed with the girls in the waiting area. "I'm looking for Blake Tobin," I asked with my hands shaking, "he was in a car accident." As the receptionist was looking for information on her computer, a nurse came over. "Yes, Blake Tobin is here but he is still in surgery." "Oh my god, in surgery?" I asked, "what kind of surgery?" The nurse responded, "Who are you? I cannot divulge any other information unless you are a spouse or family member." Just then, Dottie came up to the desk. "I am his aunt! How is he?" "Ma'am," the nurse replied, "he sustained multiple injuries from the accident. He's been in surgery for a few hours now," she continued, "I will have the doctor update you momentarily. Why don't you have a seat in the waiting area."

It had been a couple of hours, Dottie and I and the girls had been waiting patiently for any information. Dottie and I consumed several cups of coffee, and the girls ate too many snacks from the vending machines. Then a woman walked in and stopped at the nurse's station. I could barely hear her, but I did hear say Blake's name. She then turned around and was walking towards Dottie. "Aunt Dottie," she said, "what happened to Blake?" Dottie quickly replied in a bit of a snippy tone, "Oh, you came all the way out here to check on your brother? Maybe you should call him once in a while to let him know where you are!" "Auntie," the woman said, "this is not the time to hash over things." Dottie responded, "Yes, you're right." Then she looked over at me and said, "Julie, this is my niece, Amber, Blake's sister." I stood up to greet her and asked, "Oh, are you the one who used to live in the cottage?" She answered, "Yes, why, are you living there now?" I replied, "Well, I'm staying there for a while, with my girls, Mandy and Mia." She then asked, "How do you know my brother?" I hesitated then answered, "We're friends." I caught her rolling her eyes and she wasn't too friendly towards me. She then told Dottie she would be back in a while to check in on any update.

 After she left, I said to Dottie, "Well, she didn't seem too pleased to meet me." Dottie replied, "Don't let Amber get to you. She's had her share of problems and heartaches. She was Blake's wife's best friend. She was the reason Blake and Jolene got together. She doesn't want to see him with anyone else." She then put her hand on my shoulder and smiled at me. "Is there anything serious going on between the two of you?" "Oh, between Blake and I?" I said while grinning and I continued, "we have fun together and I care very much about him." "Do you love him?" Dottie asked. I took a moment before answering her, "Yes, I think I do."

 Just then the doctor came into the waiting area. We were the only ones in there, so we knew it was about Blake. Dottie and I quickly got up from our chairs and the doctor introduced himself. "I'm Doctor Stevens. You must be family of Blake's?" We nodded yes and he said, "Well, Blake has suffered significant injuries from the accident. He hemorrhaged during surgery, but we were able to stop the bleeding. He has a broken collar bone, three broken ribs which punctured his left lung, and his kidneys are severely bruised." Dottie put her hand over her mouth and took a deep breath then asked, "Will he be okay?" The doctor responded, "He'll be fine. He is incredibly lucky. Things could have been much worse. He will be admitted here into the hospital for pain management but within a few weeks, he should be ready to go home." I then asked, "Doctor, when can we see him?" "He's still in recovery but give it another half hour or so and I will have the nurse bring you all to his room." It had been longer than a half an hour but then the nurse finally came to get us and brought us to see Blake.

 When we walked into his room, I felt as if my heart sank. I couldn't stand to see him lying in bed looking so helpless and in pain. The girls propped themselves up at the end of his bed while Dottie and I pulled over chairs to sit on each side of him. Dottie began to cry as she said, "Blake is so important to me. I love him dearly." I reached over to hold her hand and said, "The doctor said he is going to be fine." We stayed with Blake for about an hour. He hadn't woken up, so we decided to leave and go back home to get some sleep. The girls were exhausted, and I knew Dottie needed to rest. The doctor said Blake may not wake up for another day or two, but he would call us when he did.

Two days later, the doctor called. Blake had finally woken up. While the girls were at school and Dottie was at the diner, I decided to drive up to the hospital to see him.

When I entered his room, I saw Amber sitting next to him on the bed. I quietly walked over. "Hi Amber," I said. She quickly turned around. "Oh, It's Julie right?" "How is he?" I asked. She replied as she was looking at him, "He's better. He was awake when I got here but fell back asleep shortly after." Just then, Blake slightly opened his eyes and softly asked, "Julie, is that you?" I went over to him and sat on the other side of the bed. I gave him a kiss on his forehead and said while holding his hand, "Yes, Blake, it's me. I'm here." Amber stormed out of the room. I told Blake I would be right back, and I ran after her.

As I was chasing her down the hallway, I yelled, "Amber! Wait!" I caught up with her in front of the elevator. I was somewhat out of breath. "What is your problem with me?" I asked. She answered rudely, "I don't have a problem with you!" I responded just a rudely, "Clearly you do!" Then she went ahead to say, "Don't you think it's ironic that on the anniversary of Tommy's death, Blake crashes his truck into a tree?!" I paused a minute as I did not know that. "What are you saying? Blake tried to commit suicide last night?" Amber looked right into my eyes and said, "You don't know him as well as you may think you do...and you certainly don't know him like I do! He's unstable and has been since his wife and son died. I'm his sister and I worry about him." I took in a deep breath then exhaled before asking, "Then why did your aunt sound like the two of you are distant from one another?" She again responded rudely, "That is none of your business!" I hesitated a second. "Look, Amber, I know you were Jolene's best friend, but it's been three years. I think it's time for Blake and for you to move on."

Just then, the elevator doors opened, and she went in and quickly pressed the button. As the doors were closing, I asked, "Can we meet later today to talk some more?" She replied, "I have nothing else to say to you." And the doors closed. I stood there for a moment, nodding my head, then headed back to Blake's room. I walked in and he was sleeping so I quietly grabbed my purse, went over to him, kissed him on the cheek and whispered the words goodbye in his ear.

On my way home, I couldn't stop thinking about what Amber said. Maybe Blake did try to kill himself. I did find it odd that the accident occurred on the same date his son had drowned. On the outside, Blake seems like such a strong yet gentle man, and I couldn't fathom him intentionally driving his truck right into a tree.

I arrived back at the cottage about an hour before the school bus would be dropping off the girls and I noticed Dottie's car in her driveway, so I decided to go over there. She answered the door and asked if I had gone to see Blake. I told her I had, and I wanted to talk to her for a bit. She let me in and brewed a fresh pot of coffee for the two of us. We sat at the kitchen table, and I started off the conversation by telling her I had run into Amber at the hospital. I then mentioned what Amber had said to me and that's when she told me. "Well, Jolene was extremely sick, and she had been suffering with the cancer for a long time. She knew she only had a matter of weeks, if not days, before she was going to die so," she paused then continued, "according to Blake, she asked him to help her die." I asked with a shocked look on my face, "What do mean help her die?" Dottie replied,

"He gave her a mixture of all of the pills she had been taking, at one time, so she would...well, you know what happened next." "Oh my god," I said in disbelief then I asked, "is that why Amber is so bitter towards him?" Dottie answered, "Yes, she still doesn't believe Jolene asked Blake to do what he did. She still thinks Blake killed her, on his own." I took a moment before responding. "That is terrible...but that's not what I was talking about." I sighed and said, "Amber made a comment to me, well, she kind of implied that what happened to Blake last night may not have been an accident." Dottie was quick to ask, "What do you mean?" I paused, "I mean, that maybe Blake tried to commit suicide last night." Dottie got right up from the table and walked over to the kitchen sink to pour out her coffee. "I didn't mean to upset you Dottie. I'm only looking for some answers." Dottie shook her head and said, "If Blake was going to kill himself, he sure would have done that the day Tommy drowned in that lake." She then came back to the table and sat down. "Julie, Blake is a good man. He has gone through more heartache in a short time than most experience in a lifetime." She continued, "I think you better focus on your future and not his past. It would be best for both of you." I agreed with Dottie and showed myself out. I didn't go to the hospital to visit Blake for the next week but then I felt myself missing him more and more, so I finally made the trip to see him.

As I walked into his room, the nurse was walking out. "Doctor Stevens just left," she said. "Blake has some good news for you." When I went over to Blake, he had a smile on his face and said, "I am so glad to see you," then he asked, "where have you been?" I paused a moment. "Um, I've had a lot of things to do for the girls at school lately." "Come sit," he said as he put his hand down on the bed. "I have good news. I am being released tomorrow." I smiled at him. I was excited since he was being released earlier than expected. "That's great!" I said but he could sense something was wrong. "Is everything okay?" he asked. "I'm just worried about you. You gave me, all of us, quite a scare." I didn't want to bring up any of the conversations I had with Amber or Dottie. It wasn't the right time, but I did ask him something I needed to know at that moment. "Blake, do you want to be in a relationship with me?" He took my hand and replied, "Of course I do. I love" he paused then said, "being with you."

The next morning, I worked at the diner for Dottie so she could pick up Blake from the hospital. I hadn't worked there much at all lately so I told her I would pick up her shifts for the following week. She wanted to take care of Blake in her home while he was still recovering rather than have him alone at his. I was happy he was staying next door since it allowed the girls and I to visit him often. I opened the Diner every day and Dottie had her hands full taking care of

Blake and making sure the girls were ready for the bus each morning. Luckily, I was able to leave the diner before the girls came home from school. I made dinner for Blake and Dottie every evening. The girls spent a lot of time sitting with Blake and he would help them with their homework. It started to feel like we were a family, including Dottie, to whom the girls had grown extremely close.

Then one morning, Dottie came over and asked me, "Julie, hon,' could you be a doll and run over to Blake's? He needs some clean t-shirts and lounge pants." "Of course," I answered as she handed me his house key. "I gotta get to the diner, the fryolator is actin'up again." The girls were in school, so I headed over to Blake's.

When I arrived, I noticed the mail piling up in his mailbox, so I brought it in and placed it on the kitchen counter. As I was rummaging through his dresser, I came across a small white envelope in one of his drawers hidden underneath his T-shirts and it had Blake's name handwritten on the front. When I turned it over, I noticed it was unsealed and I told myself not to open it, but instead, I sat on the bed and started reading the letter that was enclosed:

My dearest Blake,

Forgive me for asking you to do what you did; it was selfish of me, but I needed to stop my suffering. Thank you for your courage and strength to help me leave this world on my terms. Please do not tell Amber or Tommy as I do not want either of them to think I did not want to spend what time I had left of my life with them. I could no longer wonder when the cancer would eventually kill me. I didn't say goodbye because we will be together again one day.

Take care of Tommy. I love you both so much!

All my love,

Jolene

I could not stop my tears from flowing. My heart ached for Jolene and Blake, and for Tommy. After reading the letter, I told myself to put it back where I found it but instead, I grabbed his clothes, packed them in a small suitcase I found in his closet and tucked the letter in my purse.

When I got back home, I brought Blake's clothes to him, made him a sandwich for lunch and sat with him for a while. We talked a little about the accident but mostly about how he was feeling. He was eager to *get back to his own home which was expected to be within the next week.*

CHAPTER

EIGHT

It was a Sunday morning, and I was sitting out on the front porch getting ready to read a book when I saw Amber pull up and walk into Dottie's house. She had been there for some time. Then I looked over to see her walking towards me and I pretended to continue reading my book. As she got closer, she said, "Julie, I have something to say to you." I shut my book, got out of my chair, and asked with a smirk on my face, "What is it, Amber?" She was standing at the bottom of the stairs and I at the top. She went ahead to say, "I want to apologize for the way I've treated you. I'm sorry if I 've made you feel uncomfortable." I paused a moment and said, "I'll be right back," and quickly went inside to grab the letter. As I handed her the letter, I said, "You need to read this." She took the letter from me and sat down on the middle step. As she was reading it, she was crying. When she was finished, she folded it back up and said, "I didn't know." She wiped her tears, "I've blamed Blake for her death for so long. I knew she had more time, but I didn't realize how much she was suffering." I then sat down next to her, and she said, "I miss her so much and Tommy, too. I wish the baby could have survived." I responded with a surprised look on my face, "Baby?" She replied, "Blake didn't tell you?" "Tell me what?," I asked. "Jolene was pregnant with a little girl but when the cancer had spread throughout her body, they needed to terminate the pregnancy. She and Blake named her, Angel Rose." I sighed heavily and felt a tear run down my cheek. "How much can one person take?" Amber shook her head. "Amber, can I ask you something?" She answered, "Sure." Then I continued. "Do you think there is a chance Blake did try to kill himself?" She abruptly stood up. "Julie, what I said to you that day at the hospital was out of line! The pain Blake has endured in his life has not made him weak, it's made him stronger!" She paused a minute, "besides, he would never do that to me and Dottie...and not to you." She then sat back down next to me on the step. "Do you love him?" she asked. I looked at her and said, "I do." "Well, I know he loves you, too." I eagerly asked, "Did he tell you that?" She answered, "He didn't have to. I know my brother." After some small talk, she said, "I have to get going. I picked up a shift at the diner. After all, I have to earn my room and board." I then asked, "Oh, are you staying over at Dottie's?" She replied, "For a little while...until I can find a place of my own."

As she was walking away, I said, "Hey, Amber, I would like to keep the letter just between us." She responded, "I think that would be best." That afternoon, I drove to Blake's to put the letter back where I had found it.

A week later, Blake went back to his house and felt as good as he did before the accident. The girls were in school, so he and I planned a day trip together. The weather was perfect. We had a picnic by the stream behind Dottie's property. We spent most of the day cuddling on a blanket, drinking wine, and talking. I felt I had a real connection with Blake, one I hadn't had with anyone since Jonathan. I did not mention the letter and we didn't talk about Jolene, Tommy, or the baby. He still had no idea I knew about the baby or about Jolene's death. I was trying my hardest to block all of it out and just focus on he and I and our possible future together. It was difficult to do at times because I wanted so much to console him, but I figured if the time ever came when he needed to talk about all of it, hopefully he would confide in me.

Weeks had gone by and mine and Blake's relationship was getting stronger. We and the kids spent a lot of time together. He stayed nights here and there at the cottage and the girls and I stayed at his house often, usually on the weekends. I was still working a few shifts at the diner and Amber, and I had become friends. Everything was falling into place quite nicely. There was finally some feeling of normalcy as if we had lived in this town forever and though it had been less than two years, so much had already happened.

It was a Saturday evening, and Dottie had invited all of us, Amber included, to her house for dinner. She was making a homemade Italian dinner which was my favorite meal. Apparently, Blake had told her that.

After dinner, during dessert, which was Dottie's homemade caramel pecan pie, Blake stood up at the head of the table and said, "I would like to have all of your attention, please." We all stopped talking and waited for Blake to say whatever it was he was going to say. Then suddenly, he took out of his pocket a small black velvet box. At that moment, I had an inclination as to what could be in the box. He then said, staring at me, "Julie, can you come here and stand next to me?" I was already getting emotional. As I was standing there by his side, he said, "We haven't known each other very long, but I feel a connection with you," he then looked over at the girls and smiled "and with you kids, too." The girls smiled back at him, and he continued, "I want to move ahead and see where we end up...as a family." He bent down on one knee in front of me. He opened the box and in it was a beautiful, sparkling diamond ring. He then asked as he stared into my eyes, "Julie, will you marry me?" There wasn't a dry eye in the room, well, except for the girls, they were giggling. Even Blake had tears. I paused a minute before answering him. "Yes, I will." He stood up as the girls were jumping up and down and Dottie and Amber were clapping then he wrapped his arms around me and whispered in my ear, "I love you."

We stayed at Dottie's for a little while later then Blake and the girls and I went back over to the cottage. The girls were exhausted from all of the excitement and went right to bed. Shortly after, I looked in on them and they were both fast asleep. Blake and I rushed into my bedroom and made love. Then we laid in bed, just holding each other. I was looking at my ring and asked him, "Are you sure about this?" He replied, "Of course I am." "But are you ready? With everything you've been through," He interrupted, "I wasn't planning on us getting married right away. Maybe in the next year or two." I responded, "There's no need to rush into it." He took my comment as if I were upset or angry. He sat up against the headboard of the bed. "Julie, I want to marry you. I wouldn't have proposed to you tonight if I didn't." He kissed the top of my head and continued to say, "before Jolene died, she and I talked about what life would be like for me without her. She told me she wanted me to be happy. She said what she and I had was special and she wanted me to have something special with someone else someday," he put his hand over his eyes and let out a big sigh, "she also wanted me to be with someone who would be a good mother figure for Tommy, and I see how you are with your children." "She must have been an amazing woman." I said and he replied, "She was...and you are, too." We were kissing but then I stopped and blurted out, "I read the letter." He asked, "What letter?" I said, "Um, the letter from Jolene." "You went through my things?" he asked, seeming a bit shocked and a little angry. I sat up next to him. "No, no, it wasn't like that. It was the day Dottie asked me to go over to your place to get some clean clothes for you and as I was grabbing them from your dresser, I just happened to find it." He just sat there without saying a word. I continued to say, "Blake, I know I shouldn't have even opened it, let alone read it, but a part of me is glad that I did because now I realize how much you and Jolene meant to each other and I hope one day, we can have a love like the one you had with her." He responded, "I actually forgot the letter was still in the drawer." I know he didn't mean that, he was just trying to end the conversation.

We started making love to each other again and yet again, I stopped to blurt out something else I shouldn't have. "I'm sorry about Angel Rose." He rolled over, got out of bed to put on his pants then sat on the side of the bed. "Who told you about her?" He asked. I put his shirt on and sat next to him. "It doesn't matter...I can't imagine how hard that must have been for both of you." He paused then said something I never expected to hear. "I wasn't the father." I didn't know what to say then he continued, "Jolene had a brief affair after she was diagnosed *with cancer. I knew about it, but I also knew she didn't have much time left. I just didn't want to destroy what we had." I asked, as I was rubbing his back, "Did Jolene know you knew you weren't the father?" "No," he said, "and the man she had the affair with never knew about the pregnancy." He then turned around and looked into my eyes, "I'm glad we can be honest with each other. Honesty is important to me." I put my head down as I felt I was betraying him since I hadn't at all been honest with him about my life. At that moment, I wanted to tell him everything, especially mine and the girls' real names but instead I got up and went into the bathroom to get ready for bed.*

The following morning, Blake got up early and made breakfast for all of us. He made chocolate chip pancakes for the girls and omelets for me and him. During breakfast, the four of us were laughing, joking with each other, and having great conversations. It felt like we were already a family. It was nice but I still felt extremely guilty for not being honest with Blake and I was still afraid the time would come when I would have to be.

Months had gone by. Amber was still living with Dottie and working full time at the diner. I was still picking up shifts here and there, but I had recently found out I was pregnant. Blake and I hadn't set a date for the wedding yet, but we did tell the girls, Dottie, and Amber about the pregnancy. They were all excited for us and the girls wanted so much to have a baby brother or sister. I was only about 6 weeks pregnant. Blake seemed just as excited as they were and Dottie, well, she was elated. She couldn't wait to be a great aunt, although Blake always told me since his mother died, he always considered Dottie as his mom, and he wanted the baby to think of her as a grandmother and I agreed with that. Amber was more excited for us than I thought she would be. I knew it was early in the pregnancy, but I was already thinking of names. A part of me wanted to include Tommy's name somehow or even Jolene's. By now, I was three months pregnant. I had already had two appointments with the doctor and was feeling fairly good. It had been a long time since I was pregnant, I had forgotten what it was like. The morning sickness, however, I did not forget! Blake was so attentive to me as well as to the girls. He would take them out on hikes during the weekends so I could stay in bed and rest. Before I knew it, I was seven months pregnant. Time seemed to have gone by so fast.

One day, after the kids left for school, I went to the pharmacy to pick up a prescription my doctor ordered for me to help with the morning sickness I was still experiencing. When I arrived back home, there were two pumpkins on the front steps of the cottage. They each had sort of mean faces carved on them. I immediately thought they were from Dottie since it was close to Halloween. Then, Dottie came walking over. "Well, aren't those Jack-o-lanterns cute! Did y'all carve them last night?" she asked. I quickly replied, "Uh, I thought they were from you." "Oh no," she said, "I'm not that talented." I then asked her, "Did you see who put them there?" She responded, "They were there when I got back from the diner." "Hmm," I said, "maybe they're from Blake," but I later found out they were not. I stopped dwelling on the mysterious pumpkins. Since Halloween was approaching, the girls thought they were cool decorations.

It was Thanksgiving Day, and we were having dinner at Blake's. Amber and Dottie joined us as well. Blake and I did all the cooking along with help from the girls. It was a lovely day and Blake, and I were actually trying to settle on a date for the wedding with everyone else's input, of course. After going back and forth, we had finally decided to wait until after the baby was born before setting any date in stone but ironically, I had gone into labor soon after we had finished dessert. Blake rushed me to the hospital, it was a long ride, and I was feeling extremely uncomfortable. Dottie and Amber followed behind us with the girls. I was a few weeks early, but the doctor said everything was fine and I delivered mine and Blake's son after only a few hours of labor. We both agreed to name him Timothy Thomas Tobin. I stayed in the hospital for the next couple of days and the girls were in awe of their new baby brother although immediately after the delivery, I could sense Blake was a bit distant with the baby and I think I expected that because of his memory of Tommy but it didn't take long before he bonded with his new son.

On the afternoon I arrived home from the hospital, there had been a flower arrangement delivered and left on the front porch. Blake brought the baby and the girls into the cottage as I grabbed the flowers. There was no card attached. I had no idea who they were from. Blake and Dottie both figured they must have been from someone at the diner. After about a week of Dottie asking staff and customers about the flowers, no one owned up to sending them.

Within the next few days, I received another delivery but this time it was a small box that was left in front of the door. I was the only one home at the time but didn't hear or see anyone drop it off. I brought it inside and opened it. It was a newborn-sized baby outfit in blue with little trucks on it but again, no card enclosed. Now I was starting to get a little curious and feel a bit uneasy. It didn't make sense. Why would someone not want to be acknowledged after sending a gift.

 Christmas had come and gone. The kids and I were still staying at the cottage and Blake at his cabin since the school bus did not go past his house. He spent most nights with us and was remodeling the cabin to add a room for Timmy.

 I never did find out who sent the baby outfit or the flowers. It had been a couple of months and I hadn't received any more anonymous gifts.

It was a Friday afternoon. Blake and I were sitting on the front porch waiting for the school bus to arrive. Timmy was inside napping. We then noticed a bus drive by without stopping at the end of the driveway.

A few minutes later, we saw the same bus driving in the opposite direction. Another five minutes went by and still no sign of the girls. I was beginning to worry, and Blake was trying to keep me calm. Dottie was coming up the driveway and I rushed over to her car, screaming, "Dottie! Are the girls with you?!" She quickly parked and jumped out of the car, sounding a bit panicked herself. "No, was I supposed to pick them up from school today?" "No," I said frantically, "but they weren't on the school bus!" I started to run around the yard, yelling both of their names.

Suddenly, a car pulled up to the end of the driveway and Mandy and Mia came out from the doors of the back seat. I began yelling at them. "Where have you girls been? I have been waiting for you! Why weren't you on the bus!" A young woman got out of the car and stood next to the driver's side door. "You must be Mrs. Banks," she said in a pleasant voice. "It's Ms." I replied harshly. "I am Miss Miller. Mandy and Mia's reading teacher." She continued, "Mandy and Mia both volunteered along with other children to help with a class project after school today." I was still angry. "Girls, get in the house and start your homework...and be quiet, Timmy's napping!" Miss Miller proceeded to say, "The girls both tried calling you from school as did I, but your phone went straight to voicemail, and we left text messages, but you didn't respond to any of them." "Well, I didn't receive any calls or texts!" I said as I was searching through my purse for my phone...but it wasn't in there. I then said, "I'll be right back," and ran into the cottage to find my phone turned off and on the counter, plugged into the charger. When I turned it on, there were several missed calls along with voice and text messages.

I came back out with my phone in my hand, looked directly at the teacher and said, "I apologize, Miss Miller. I never realized I didn't have my phone with me." She opened the driver's side door and as she was about to get in, I asked her, "Miss Miller, do you have children of your own?" She answered, "No, I do not." 'Well," I said, "then you don't know what it's like to think your children are missing." "No, I do not...but I can tell you that Mandy and Mia are good kids. They are a pleasure to have in class and I would want to make sure they are safe, too." I kindly thanked her for driving the girls home. She smiled and drove away.

When I turned around Blake was standing there. "Julie, what got into you? I've never seen you like that before." I sighed. "I just worry about the girls, that's all."

That evening, Dottie offered to take the girls to her house for the night. I reluctantly agreed but the girls really wanted to go. It was getting late, so I decided to head to bed. I had called the girls earlier to say goodnight. Just as soon as my head hit the pillow, I heard a noise. It sounded like someone was trying to open the front door then suddenly, there was a loud knock. I quicky jumped out of bed but slowly and quietly walked towards the door. There was a knock again and I was hesitant to open the door, but I did just enough to see who it was. I was shocked and frantically asked, "What are you doing here? How did you find me?" It was Nancy. She responded, "Well, that's no way to treat your good friend. After all, I was almost your sister-in-law." I asked, "What are you talking about?" I had no idea what she meant by that comment. I tried to close the door but before I could, she pushed it wide open and came right in, slamming the door behind her. She was yelling, "Where are my brother's girls?! Where are my nieces?!" I asked, "You're Jonathan's sister?" She yelled, "Yes, I am!" I yelled back at her, "I am not telling you, but they are not here!" Then I ran into my bedroom to grab my phone on the nightstand and call Blake, but she followed me, and I couldn't close the door quickly enough. As I was calling Blake, she pushed me on the bed and threw my phone onto the floor. I was screaming and hoping Blake would answer my call. We were wrestling on the bed for a while then she pinned me down and I couldn't get up. Her hands were wrapped tightly around my neck. I was gasping for air, struggling to breathe. I could barely reach the knife I had hidden under my pillow, I put it there every night before falling asleep, but I managed to grab hold of it and within seconds, I stabbed Nancy in the neck. She stopped choking me and I pushed her off the bed. Just as she fell to the floor, Blake came running in, screaming my name. He grabbed me and carried me out of the cottage and said, "I heard your screams on the phone, so I called 911 and headed right over here." Outside there were police cars and ambulances with their blue and red lights flashing. As we were standing on the porch, the EMTs were rolling Nancy out on the stretcher, and I saw Dottie holding the girls in the driveway. The girls were crying. Then a police officer came up to me. "Are you Sara Frost?" he asked. I looked at Blake before answering, "Yes, I am," then I turned to Blake and said, "I am so sorry." The officer then said, "We need you to come down to the station to answer some questions." Blake intervened, "Officer, can this wait? I will bring her in first thing in the morning." The officer replied, "Sure, it can wait," then he said as he was looking at me, "but I think you should get checked out at the hospital, you have significant bruising around your neck." "I'm fine," I said, "I just need to be with my girls right now." As the officer walked away, I held Blake's hand and said, "I will explain everything to you tomorrow, I promise." Then I went running over to the girls.

 The police and EMTs had left. It was just Dottie, the girls and me, standing in the driveway as Blake went to lock up the cottage. I looked at Dottie and said, "I am sorry for all of this. I haven't been honest with you." She put her arms around me and said, "It's okay. We don't need to talk about it right now. You and the girls need to get some sleep and I think it would be best if you all slept at my house tonight." I slept with the girls in one room and Blake slept in another.

 The next morning, the girls and I were awakened by a wonderful aroma of Dottie's home cooked country breakfast. As we were walking down the stairs, I could hear Blake's voice. When I entered the kitchen, he came over and hugged me and the girls. I didn't say anything. I told the girls to sit down at the table and wait for breakfast. Dottie poured me a cup of coffee and gave the girls orange juice. The five of us sat down to eat but there were few words spoken and nothing said about the night before.

 After breakfast, Blake asked, "Are you ready to go to the police station?" I grabbed my purse and said,

"Let's go and get this over with." On the way, which was quite a long distance, Blake asked, "Why did that officer ask if you were Sara Frost last night?" I cleared my throat then responded, "Um, I told you I would explain everything to you today and I will but first I want to talk with the police." "I understand," he said, "but I need you to be honest with me, tell me everything, no holding back," he then gently grabbed my hand, "I need to know the person I fell in love with." I just gave him a little smile and stared out the window for the rest of the ride.

When we arrived at the police station, I was starting to feel nervous and anxious. Blake said he would wait out in the truck for me, no matter how long it took. When I walked in, an officer at the front desk asked, "Ma'am, can I help you?" I replied with my voice shaking a bit, "I'm Sara Frost." The officer then said, sounding a bit eager, "Let me get the detective for you."

A few minutes later, a man walked over to me. He was wearing a beige colored suit jacket with his tie undone and denim jeans. He said, as he held out his hand to shake mine, "Ms. Frost, thank you for coming in. I'm Detective Rutland. Why don't we go into my office and chat." I followed him to his office. He told me to have a seat and left for a minute but returned with a cup of water for me. "I have a lot of questions for you. I hope you don't mind but this may take a while." I said, "That's fine." He asked, "Did you know Nancy Burrows prior to the incident last night?" I took a deep breath before answering him. "Uh, yes, I did." I then explained, "but I hadn't spoken to her for quite a long time, and I had no idea who she really was. She went by the name Nancy Marsh." "The detective said, "That was her married name before she was divorced," he continued to say, "well, you've been in hiding for quite a while." he said. I replied, "Three years, eleven months and twelve days, to be exact." I then had to ask, "Is she alright?" Detective Rutland hesitated for a moment, "She died on the way to the hospital." I quickly said frantically, "I did not mean to kill her! It was self-defense. You have to believe me!" He said, "I do. I know Ms. Burrows intentionally set out to kill you. My partner and I found evidence that she had been looking for you for quite some time." He then asked, "what was your relationship with Derek Sands?" I didn't answer him right away. "Um, he was my boyfriend. The night I left him, was the night I read a text message on his cell phone from Nancy telling him she was going to come grab my girls the next morning...and I couldn't let her take them!" He said, "I understand Nancy is the sister of the late Jonathan Burrows, Is that correct?" I took a deep breath and replied, "Yes, yes she is... or was but again, I didn't know that until last night." Then the detective asked, "Was Mr. Burrows your children's biological father?" I put my head down then looked up at him. "Yes...but he died in a car accident when I was just three months pregnant...I never told his family I gave birth to his children. In fact, the day of the accident, was the day I found out I was pregnant." I started to cry, "I never even got the chance to tell him." He looked a bit confused. "Do you think Derek knew the whole time *you were with him, and he was working with the family to take your kids away from you?" I didn't respond. Then he said, "Ms. Frost, I can't have Mr. Sands answer any questions because he is deceased." I was in shock then asked, "Derek's dead?" Detective Rutland proceeded to say, "He was found in his car a couple weeks ago, with a gunshot to his head," he continued, "the murder weapon was found a few days later, in a nearby dumpster with Nancy's fingerprints all over it." "Oh my god!" was all I could say. Then after a few minutes of silence, I asked, "Detective Rutland, should I still be worried about his family trying to take my children away from me?" He then showed me a photo. "Do you know who this woman is?" he asked. I looked at the photo for a couple minutes then it came to me. "Yes, that's Jonathan's mother." "Oh," he said, "then you know Linda Burrows?" he asked while sounding surprised. "No, I don't," I said but then continued, "I stood behind all the guests at Jonathan's funeral service and never got a clear view of all his family members but at the time, I assumed this woman was his mother since she looked to be the oldest standing next to the casket." Detective Rutland asked, "You went to his funeral, pregnant?" I answered in a bit of a snappy tone, "As I said, I was only three months pregnant and wasn't even showing yet." I then continued to say, "and I felt it was the right thing to do to pay my respects to my fiancé." He responded,*

"May I ask why his family didn't know about the two of you?" I sighed. "Jonathan told me he had been estranged from his family for years…he never spoke much about them," I continued, "Jonathan was a wonderful man, so I figured if he had issues with his family, it was because of them, not him. He was a calm and gentle man who I loved very much." Detective Rutland then stood up from his desk. "Ms. Frost, can I get you more water, or some coffee or tea?" "No, thank you, I'm fine." I answered. He then said, "Okay, I will be right back." He was gone for about fifteen minutes then returned. "How did Nancy and Derek know each other?" I started biting at my fingernails. "Um, I don't know." 'Well," he said, "you told me you saw a text message from Nancy on Derek's cell phone…I need you to tell me the truth. Otherwise, I cannot help you." I closed my eyes for a few seconds. "Okay, I had met Nancy at a cafe a few years ago. The two of us were standing in line waiting for a long time to place our orders and we got to talking which led to exchanging cell phone numbers and a few days later, we made plans to meet for lunch at the same café." He asked, "So, you met her for lunch?" "Yes," I replied, "we had lunch then started meeting weekly at a yoga class." He seemed frustrated. "Why are you just mentioning all of this now?" I replied, "I don't know but I will tell you, I did not know she was Jonathan's sister, well, not really but I suspected something wasn't right."

"What do you mean?" he asked. I responded, "It wasn't until I invited Nancy back to my apartment, well, mine and Derek's apartment, one day after yoga class," I continued, "the girls were at home with Derek at the time. After she had been there for a while, we had dinner and drinks, and she noticed a photo of Jonathan and I on one of the end tables in the living room." Detective Rutland interrupted, "So, Derek knew the kids were Jonathan's? Did he know Jonathan?" I answered him after a big sigh. "No, he didn't know him, and I never really talked about Jonathan, but he knew the girl's father was killed in an accident, our relationship started as a one-night stand," I continued on, "I walked into the living room and saw Nancy holding the framed photo in her hands, just staring at it." I cleared my throat, "she then asked me who the man was in the photo, and I told her it was my fiancé who had passed away in a car accident. I should have suspected something when she told me about having a brother who also died in a car accident around the same time, but I really should have known there was a connection when she later made a comment, with a tear rolling down her cheek, about how much my girls looked like the man in the photo." "What did you do after that?" he asked. I quickly answered, "I stopped going to Yoga class and didn't answer any of her calls or text messages. But then one day, about a month later, I saw her and Derek in front of a hotel...in each other's

arms...and that's when I began wondering if the two of them were having an affair." Detective Rutland put down his pen. "Why didn't you confront them?" I put my hand on my forehead. "What was I going to say? I didn't really want to know. I was scared to even bring it up with him. Derek had his moments when he would drink excessively or smoke too much weed and I had to keep myself and my girls away from him until he sobered up." Then he asked, "Did he ever hit your or the children?" "Oh no," I quickly replied, "well, he would threaten to discipline the girls if they didn't listen to him and I knew what that meant...because he hit me once in a while, usually when he drank too much or smoked marijuana...but I knew he didn't mean to. When he wasn't drinking, he was a great man. He treated me and my children good," I added, "when I saw the two of them together that day in front of the hotel, I forgot all about the day Nancy was at the apartment."

Then, the office phone rang, and Detective Rutland answered it. "Okay, thanks for the information." He hung up and looked right at me for a minute. "We have results from DNA samples taken from both Derek Sands and Nancy Burrows," he paused a minute, "and they are both a match to your fiancé's DNA." I was in disbelief. "What?" I quickly asked, "are you telling me that Derek was also Jonathan's sibling?" "They are half siblings, different fathers, that explains why they didn't have the same last name," he replied, "and we believe the two of them were both scheming to take custody of yours and Jonathan's children for quite some time," he then added, "I also believe your first encounter with Nancy at the café was pre-planned." I then had to ask, "Detective Rutland, am I in any trouble?" He paused briefly then responded, "Criminally, no...but you have been on the run with false identities...but I also know you were just trying to keep your girls with you." I then asked, "What do I do now?" He replied, "You continue living your new life, keeping your kids safe and making sure they are well taken care of, and I suggest you immediately file the proper paperwork to legally change your names," he added, "however, if you had contacted the police rather than run away, all of this could have ended differently. Law enforcement would have intervened and could have done something to protect you and your kids." I nodded by head, "You're right and now I wish I had gone to the police first." We both stood up and as we were leaving his office, he said, "I will be sure to contact you if I have any more questions or receive any other information you should be aware of."

 He walked me out the front door of the building and as we were standing on the front steps, he said, holding his hand out to shake mine, "Well, Ms. Frost, it was nice to meet you." I quickly responded while shaking his hand, "Please, call me Julie...Julie Banks...Sara Frost doesn't exist anymore." We smiled at one another, and I walked down the stairs and over to Blake's truck parked next to the curb.

 As soon as I got into Blake's truck, I reached over and kissed him, "Can we go somewhere private to talk?" I was ready to tell him everything from the beginning. He said, "I know the perfect place." and we ended up at the beautiful stream in the woods behind Dottie's property. We were there for hours, sitting on the rock we had stood on before. I tried my hardest not to cry but there were times, I just couldn't control myself. Blake was so understanding however, we did both agree to not tell Dottie the truth until things settled so in the meantime, Dottie just assumed the attack in the cottage was a random incident. Before long, we were both laughing and talking about other things, good things. I knew at that moment; I could see us spending the rest of our lives together, extremely happy. During the next several weeks, Blake and I spent a lot of time together and with the kids, too. Everything seemed perfect. We were soon to be living in the cabin, all together as a family. The girls were excited. I was finally starting a fresh new life for me and them but one without constantly looking over my shoulder.

We were all moved into the cabin. Blake and I had been busy redecorating his, or should I say "our" house. The girls were attending a new school not far from the school they were going to when we lived in the cottage, but we had to drop them off and pick them up every day. Amber and Dottie helped as needed. I was working a few shifts at Dot's Diner as a thank you to Dottie for all she had done for us. I continued to call myself Julie and the girls decided they wanted to continue to be Mandy and Mia from now on as they had both gotten used to their new names. So, we were now Julie, Mandy, and Mia Banks.

It was a Sunday afternoon, and we were getting ready to head out to Dottie's house for a barbecue. She had just rented her cottage out to an older, single woman the week before. I had not met her yet, but Dottie told us the woman would be joining us at the cook-out, and I knew Dottie was a good judge of character.

When we arrived in the back yard, the kids ran over to Dottie and gave her a big hug as they had not seen her for a couple of weeks. They referred to her as Grandma Dottie now and I was fine with it. After all, I had robbed them of ever knowing their real grandmother, meaning Jonathan's mother.

There was a woman sitting at the picnic table. She looked to be in her late sixties, with dark brown hair and piercing blue eyes. Jonathan had eyes like that. In fact, she looked a lot like him, then I realized from seeing her briefly at Jonathan's funeral and the photo the detective had shown me that it was Linda Burrows, Jonathan's mother. I was in shock and a bit scared at first. I wasn't sure what to expect next. She got up and began walking over to me. I admit I was nervous. "Hello," she said in a friendly voice, "You must be Julie." I responded with a grin, pretending I didn't know who she was, just as she pretended to not know who I was. I certainly didn't think it was a coincidence that she was there. "Yes, I am and those are my girls," I said as I was pointing to them, "Mandy and Mia." She then said as she was looking over at them, "Awe, twins, they are beautiful." "Thank you," I said. Then I introduced her to Blake as he was holding Timmy, "This is my fiancé, Blake and our son." "Well, Blake," she said, "I've heard a lot about you from your aunt Dottie, well, she has spoken very highly of both of you." Dottie then came over and said, "Oh, I see you have met my new tenant, Linda." I didn't say anything to Dottie or Blake about knowing who she was, and I just kept myself calm and was cordial.

After some small talk, we all went over to the picnic table and sat down to continue conversations and I noticed Linda constantly looking over at me but surprisingly, it wasn't uncomfortable. It was sort of nice because I could see Jonathan in her, and she spoke just as softly as he used to.

We were all getting along quite well. Blake was telling his jokes all afternoon. He could be really funny at times, and he always made the girls laugh.

After we ate, I put Timmy to bed in the house and Blake built a fire for all of us to sit around. It felt as if we were camping, and the girls loved it since they had never been camping before. Dottie brought out stuff for smores and Linda showed the girls how to make them. Both Mandy and Mia seemed to really bond with her. It was a lovely evening had by all.

The next morning, detective Rutland called me. I hadn't heard from him since I talked to him at the station. He asked if he could come by the house or if I could meet him at the police station, so I opted to meet him there. Blake stayed home with the kids, and I drove his truck to the station.

When I arrived, Detective Rutland was waiting for me at the front entrance. "Julie, please, come on in, let's go into my office," he said. I asked, "Is everything all right?" "We'll talk in here," he said as he opened his office door. We both sat down, and he pulled out the photo of Jonathan's mother he had shown me before and asked," Do you remember our conversation about this woman?" I quickly responded, "Yes, I do! I was with her yesterday at a cook-out." He took a sip of his coffee, "What do mean, you were with her?" I replied, "She is actually staying at the cottage I used to live in." Detective Rutland seemed a bit confused. "Did you tell her who you are and that you know who she is?" I responded, "Of course not, at least not yet. Detective Rutland, I can't keep hiding from Jonathan's family. I know she must have been looking for me and she found me. I need to start being honest with everyone and I must say, she seems like a genuinely nice woman, and I actually feel a little sorry for her." He replied, "Well, you're right, she was looking for you. In fact, she hired a private investigator a while back to search for you and you can imagine how difficult it must have been to find you under your assumed name, but I am convinced Linda Burrows had nothing to do with the scheme to kidnap your kids or knew anything about what Derek and Nancy were up to and I've done a background check on her and it's clean." I then did wonder how she knew about me, but I also felt it was time, since the girls were older now and I had my new life with Blake, to have some kind of relationship with her. It was the right thing for me to do. "Detective Rutland," I said, "I do not feel threatened by Jonathan's mother, and I just want all of what I've *gone through to have a happy ending, for me and my children, and if that means I need to let Linda in our lives, then so be it." "I agree with you," Detective Rutland said, "and I wanted to tell you that I spoke with Linda Burrows, and she said she just wants to get to know you and her grandchildren. She seemed genuine and I wouldn't be at all worried about her intentions." I then asked, a bit surprised, "You spoke with her?" He took a sip of his coffee, "Yes, she came into the station the other day. That's how I found out about the private investigator. This woman has lost all three of her children, horrifically, I might add. I believe she needs closure but at the same time, I think she needs to have someone in her life, especially the daughter-in-law she would have had and her grandchildren she hasn't had the chance to know."*

As I was driving home, I was thinking about my conversation with Detective Rutland and found myself wanting and needing to get to know Linda even more. It was time to move on with my life, so I decided to drive to the diner and finally tell Dottie the truth. When I walked in, she was quite busy, so I sat at a booth near the back and waited for her. Amber was working so she brought over a cup of coffee to me. We chatted for a few minutes then Dottie came and sat down with me. "Hey honey, what brings you in here today?" she asked. I exhaled deeply then replied, "Um, Dottie, I need to talk to you. Is now a good time?" "Sure," she answered, "Amber can manage things for a bit. What's on your pretty little mind?" I took a sip of my coffee before responding, "I haven't been honest with you, and I feel I owe you the truth now with everything that has happened." I cleared my throat and continued, "my name is not Julie Banks…it's Sara…Sara Frost and my girls' real names are Kailey and Kya." Dottie didn't look too surprised. "Well, I knew you must have been running away from somethin'…Hell, hon' how do you think I ended up here? I didn't want to live in a small town like this, but I had to get away from my ex-husband, he hit me one last time." "Oh, I'm sorry, I didn't know," I said. She replied, "I don't really talk about it much, it was a long time ago." I then asked, "Is he still around?" "Oh no," she chuckled, "he died a few years back, he was nothin' but a drunk." "Well," I said, "I wasn't running away from an abusive, drunk ex-husband…well, not an ex-husband anyway." Tears started to fill my eyes. "You've done so much for me and my kids, I feel awful for not telling you the truth the day I meant you." She placed her hand over mine. "Honey, you did what you needed to do. Your girls come first and now your son does, too." I then took a deep breath and exhaled slowly. "Dottie, there's more." I continued, "Your new tenant, Linda, is my ex-fiancé's mother…Kailey and Kya's grandmother." She took a moment to respond. "Oh, I had no idea…is that okay that she is staying in the cottage?" I nodded my head, "Yes, it's fine. It's time I let the girls know their grandmother." She was silent for a minute before asking, "Have you told Blake about all this?" I replied, "Yes, we talked, and he knows everything" then I said to myself, well, he really didn't know EVERYTHING, and I continued, "but I haven't told you everything, especially about the night I was attacked." Dottie interrupted, "Honey, I don't need to know anything. As long as you, Blake and the kids are all safe, that's all I need to know." I said to her, "I just want the girls, and Timmy and I to continue living our lives here...with Blake and with you. I don't want to look back. I want to keep being Julie and the girls want to stay with their new names. I am filing the necessary paperwork to make that happen." Dottie smiled and said, "Well, I think Julie Tobin has a nice ring to it."

 After legally changing mine and the girls' names, Blake and I finally began planning our wedding. We thought it would be nice to have it on Dottie's property, since that is where we first met. The girls were extremely excited to help with the planning. It would be a small ceremony followed by a catered buffet-style reception. Dottie wanted a few workers from the diner to attend along with a couple friends of hers and Linda asked if she could invite a close friend of hers as well. Blake was inviting two or three friends from the tavern and a guy he once worked with a few years ago whom I had never met.

I was shopping at the local market. As I was walking out to my car holding a bag of groceries, I heard a man yell behind me, "Sara!" I didn't turn around and continued walking to the car. He yelled again, "Sara, it's me!" I stopped and turned around. I couldn't believe who it was. It was him. It was my brother, Ben. He looked the same as he did the last time I saw him, only years older. I dropped my bag of groceries on the ground and ran up to him. We tightly embraced each other and were both crying. "I've missed you so much," he said. I said, "I've missed you, too."

After a few minutes holding one another, we both let go and stared at each other for a minute. "It really is you," I said while wiping the tears off my face, "how did you find me?" He quickly replied, "I've been searching for you for a long time." I smiled at him then asked, "How is Dad?" He paused a moment. "Dad passed away." "When? How?" I asked. His eyes welled up. "About a year and half ago. It was sudden. A heart attack killed him." I didn't say anything. "He wasn't a bad man, you know," he said. I felt myself getting anxious. "Dad left me Ben! He took YOU with him!" He responded, "You were so young, and he didn't think he could take care of you like mom could." "Oh," I said in an aggravated tone, "and a hell of a job she did. Mom overdosed when I was eleven and I had to live with Grandma then she died, and I was on my own when I was a teenager." He put his arm on my shoulder, "I'm sorry Sara." I told him, "I'm not Sara anymore. I'm Julie...Julie Banks...soon to be Tobin." "You're getting married?" he asked. "Yes, next month," I continued, "what about you? Are you married?" He replied, "Uh, yea, well, not really...my divorce will be final in a couple months." "Any kids?" I asked. "No," he replied, "just a couple of dogs to fight over." I nodded my head. "I have two daughters and a son." "Wow!" he said, "I guess we have a lot to catch up on." "I guess we do," I said, and we smiled at each other. "When can we meet again?" he eagerly asked and I eagerly replied, "Let me talk with my fiancé, Blake. Maybe you can come over for dinner tomorrow to meet him and the kids." He nodded and said, "Yes, I would like that." "Ok, why don't you give me your number and I will call you in the morning." I handed him my cell phone and he added his number into my contacts then he looked over at the groceries on the ground. "Let me help you pick those up," he said as we walked over to them. As he handed me the bag, he looked at me for a moment and said sincerely, "I'm really glad I found you." I looked at him and smiled, "I'm glad you did, too."

That evening, after dinner when the kids were asleep, I told Blake about Ben. I hadn't told him before I even had a brother and I never told him about my childhood. He wasn't angry but he was upset with me since I had still been keeping secrets from him, so I finally did tell him everything about my family. He agreed to have Ben over. I didn't get any sleep that night. I couldn't stop thinking about my father. A part of me was sad that he died because I would never have the chance to see him again and a part of me was glad he was dead because of what he did to me…but also, a small part of me knew deep down, he must have thought he was doing the right thing at the time.

After tossing and turning all night, the morning finally came. I was up earlier than usual and eager to call Ben, which I did before I poured myself a cup of coffee. When I called it went straight to voicemail. I called again and it went to voicemail. I waited a few minutes and tried again but, again, it went right to voicemail. I left a message for him to call me then I decided to text him. GOOD MORNING, BEN, IT'S YOUR SISTER. I LEFT A MESSAGE ON YOUR VOICEMAIL. GIVE ME CALL.

It was almost noon, and I hadn't heard from Ben yet. So, I tried calling him again, but he didn't answer. This time it just kept ringing. I texted him again. BEN, IT'S YOUR SISTER AGAIN. CALL ME OR TEXT ME BACK.

Now it was five o'clock and I still had not heard from Ben. Blake had just come home from work. I was sitting out on the porch. He walked up and gave me a kiss. "Hey honey, what did you decide to make for dinner tonight?" I quickly answered him. "He's not coming." "Why not?" he asked. "I don't know. I haven't been able to reach him all day," I said. "Did you leave a message?" "Of course, I did," I responded with a snippy tone, "I left voicemails and text messages." I started to cry, and Blake bent down to give me a hug. "I'm sure there's a good explanation, you'll probably hear from him soon."

Three days had passed, and I had left more voicemails and text messages for Ben, but I still hadn't heard from him. Then, on the fourth day, I went back to the market. As I was at the register, I saw Ben walk in. I paid the cashier and rushed out of the store with my head down, but Ben noticed me and yelled my name. "Sara!" I quickly turned around and yelled back at him. "Don't call me that!" As I was walking to my car, he followed. I opened my trunk and threw in my grocery bags. I then walked to the driver's side and opened the door. He stood behind me and pleaded, "Please, let me explain." I said to him, "There is nothing to explain, Ben!"

As I was just about ready to get into the car, he closed my door. "Look, I know I should have returned your calls and messages, but I guess I wasn't ready after all" I interrupted him, "Weren't ready for what?" He replied, "I wasn't ready to talk about what happened." I put my hands up and said in a loud voice, "YOU searched for me! YOU found me!" He quickly responded, "I know and now I'm ready to talk about everything. I want to know all about you. I want to meet my nieces and nephew and your fiancé." I opened my car door but before I got in, I said something to him I didn't mean to say. "I was doing fine not knowing anything about you!" I got into my car, slammed the door shut, started the car, and sped off.

As I was driving away, I could see him in the rearview mirror standing in the middle of the parking lot watching me leave. As I was about to turn onto the main road, I heard a loud screeching sound and when I looked into the mirror again, I saw a car stopped with a man lying on the ground in front of it. I parked the car and quickly got out. There were several people standing around the man and as I got closer, I could see that it was Ben. I started screaming his name while running to him. I leaned over him and yelled for someone to call 911. His eyes were barely open, and he said to me in a faint whisper, "I'm sorry Sis," then he closed his eyes and that is when I remembered he used to call me Sis when we were kids.

Soon, the ambulance came to rush him to the nearest hospital, and I followed behind. I waited a while at the hospital before I was able to obtain any information on Ben's condition but eventually, the doctor came into the waiting area to update me. "I'm Dr. Cole. Are you Ben Frost's sister?" he asked. I told him I was, and he said, "Ben is out of surgery. He has suffered many serious injuries, but we were able to stop the internal bleeding. That is all the information

I can give you at this time." I began to whimper. "Can I see him?" The doctor responded, "Yes, but he is in a coma. I will have the nurse take you to his room."

When I walked into Ben's room, I let out a heavy sigh and started to cry. He looked so helpless lying there with tubes going in and out of him. I pulled a chair up next to him and took hold of his hand. I said to him, "Ben, it's me, Sis...you have to wake up, you cannot leave me again. Not again." Just then, a woman walked into the room. She looked at me and asked, "Who are you?" I stood up and answered her. "I'm Ben's sister." She came over to me and put her hand out to shake mine. "Oh, you're Sara. Ben has talked a lot about you." I was quite surprised to hear that. "He has? And please call me Julie. I'm no longer Sara." She looked a bit confused. "I'm Leah...Ben's wife...well, almost ex." I nodded and said, "I heard." Leah then pulled a chair up to Ben's bedside. She reached over and gave him a kiss on his cheek, and I could hear her whisper, "Honey, it's me, Leah. I'm here." I thought that was a little odd since they were getting divorced. I was pacing the room when Leah asked, "Do you want to get a cup of coffee at the cafeteria with me?" I said yes and we both walked down to the hospital café. Neither of us said anything to each other on the way. We ordered our coffees and Leah took out cash to pay for both of them. We then found a small table to sit at.

After a few minutes of silence, I started the conversation by asking her why she was divorcing Ben. "Ben is a really great guy, and we had a good marriage but over the past couple of years, we realized we each wanted different things in our lives." I could see she was getting a little choked up as she said, "I will always love him." A few minutes later, she cleared her throat. "Can I ask you a question?" I said, "Sure." "Why did you change your name?" she asked curiously. I paused a moment before answering. "I just didn't want to be who I was anymore."

After a couple minutes with neither one of us saying anything, I thought I'd change the subject, so I blurted out, "I'm getting married." "You are, when?" Leah asked, sounding excited for me. "In a few weeks...but I think I'm going to postpone the wedding." "Why?" she asked. I sighed. "Because I want Ben to be there...I need him to be there...he's all I have left in my family, other than my children, of course." She took a deep breath then said, "Julie, you know there is a fifty percent chance of Ben not surviving this, right? That is what Dr. Cole said." I looked at her with a bit of a smirk. "Well, then he has a fifty percent chance of surviving." She nodded her head up and down. "You're right, and I'm praying that he does." She stood up and said, "I really need to get going. I have a Zoom meeting for work in an hour." As she grabbed her purse, she said, "I won't be able to come here tomorrow until late afternoon, will you be here?" I replied, "I will be here in the morning." "Ok, maybe I will see you the day after...it was very nice meeting you, Julie," she said sincerely. I responded in the same manner, "Yes, you too...oh, and thank you for the coffee." "Anytime," she said as she walked away.

 For the next couple of days, there had been no change in Ben's condition. I hadn't seen Leah since the morning when we had coffee together. She and I were visiting Ben on different schedules.

It was a Friday morning, I woke up early, took a quick shower, got dressed and headed back up to the hospital to see Ben.

When I entered his room, the nurse was looking at his chart. I asked her, "How is he?" She looked up at me and said, "He had a rough night. His blood pressure and oxygen levels were dangerously low, but we were able to stabilize him." She closed his chart and said, "Dr. Cole will discuss it further with you when he comes in."

As she was walking out of the room, she saw that I was moving a chair over to his bedside. "If you need anything, just press the call button." "I will, thank you," I replied. I sat down next to him, placed his hand over mine and started talking to him. "Ben, it's Sis...you need to get better, do you hear me?...I need you...you're my big brother and I want you in my life again." I began to cry and said, "I love you, Ben." Then I turned my head away from him to look out the window and right at that moment, I felt my hand being squeezed. I immediately turned back around and started saying in a loud voice but not screaming, "Ben! If you can hear me, squeeze my hand again, give me a sign...anything! Come on, Ben, please!"

and then I saw his index finger move a little. Leah was just walking into the room as I was pressing the call button. "Leah!" I said frantically, "Ben squeezed my hand! He squeezed my hand and moved his finger!" "Oh my god!" she replied as she ran over to him. Then the nurse came in. "Do you need something?" "Yes," I answered, "yes, he squeezed my hand and moved his finger!" The nurse said, "Ok, I will page Dr. Cole." About five minutes later, Dr. Cole walked in along with the nurse and said, "The nurse told me you think Mr. Frost squeezed your hand." I responded to him with an arrogant tone. "His name is Ben, you can call him Ben and I don't think he did, I know he did!" "Well," Dr. Cole said, "let's take a look." He began examining Ben, looking in his eyes with a light and checking his vitals. He then held his hand and began talking to him. "Ben, this is Dr. Cole. If you can hear me, squeeze my hand." There was silence as we were all waiting for something to happen.

After a couple more minutes, Dr. Cole continued. "Ben, if you can hear me, move your fingers." Still nothing was happening. "I know what I felt and what I saw," I said aloud. Then the doctor explained, "It's not uncommon for a coma patient to experience muscle spasms or nerve movements." I abruptly interrupted him, "But I" then Leah interrupted me, "Julie, let the doctor finish." Doctor Cole cleared his throat and continued. "As I was saying, I am not doubting that you felt a squeeze or saw a twitch of a finger but there has not been any brain activity since Ben arrived here at the hospital. The next seventy-two hours are critical. I wish I could tell you he is going to pull through this, but we just don't know. It's up to him now," he turned to the nurse and said, "his vitals are stable. Page me if anything changes." He walked out of the room and the nurse soon left as well.

It was quiet and I was just standing there staring at Ben. Leah placed her hand on my shoulder and said, "Why don't you and I go grab an early lunch, at the cafeteria. I didn't eat breakfast and I could go for a nice salad and a hot cup of soup." "Ok," I replied, "I skipped breakfast, too." While we were having lunch, we were telling each other stories about Ben, though I didn't have many since we were apart for so long, but I enjoyed hearing Leah talk about him. It made me feel as if I was getting to know him. I also talked a lot about my kids, and she talked about their dogs.

After we finished eating, we both headed back up to Ben's room, but when we got there, the door was closed and Dr. Cole along with several nurses were in the room surrounding him. Then a nurse rushed out of the room, and I stopped her and asked, "What's wrong? What's happening?" She said, "There's been a code blue, they are working on him now." And she quickly ran away. Leah and I just stood in front of the door until another nurse came over to us. "Ladies," she said in a hurry, "I need you both to go to the waiting area. The doctor will see you when he's finished with the patient."

 We waited for over thirty minutes. Leah and I weren't saying anything to each other, we were both silent then Dr. Cole came into the waiting area. We both stood up and I asked, "How's Ben?" He looked at both of us and we could tell it wasn't good. "Ben suffered a brain aneurysm. It's quite common with these types of brain injuries. We did everything we could, we just" I interrupted him, "Are you saying Ben didn't make it? He's gone?" I started crying hysterically and Leah put her arms around me while the doctor continued. "I'm sorry. There was nothing else we could do. You may see him if you'd like before we transport him to the morgue." After Dr. Cole left, Leah hugged me and said, "We're going to be okay." I stepped away from her and said in a not so nice tone, "I'm not going to be okay! You're going to be okay, after all, you were divorcing him!" She quickly responded, "That's not fair! I still loved him!" She grabbed her purse from the chair and said, "I'm leaving! I need to get out of this damn hospital!" and I just let her go without saying another word but before I left, I did go to see Ben one last time.

It was the day of Ben's funeral, and I hadn't spoken with Leah other than once over the phone to confirm the arrangements. It was a small service held where Ben and Leah lived which was in another state about five hours away. Blake and I attended while Amber stayed at the house for the night with the kids because we didn't want to make the long trip twice in one day. We reserved a hotel room not far from where Leah was staying.

The service was lovely, and it was a warm and sunny afternoon. After the burial, Leah invited a few guests back to her and Ben's home, well, the home they spent many years in when they were together. She included me and Blake. The house was beautiful. It was modern and newly renovated. There were pictures of Ben and Leah everywhere. After all of the guests left, it was just Blake, Leah, and I. It was a little awkward at first but then Blake started a conversation by asking her about the renovation of the home.

After a while, I asked Blake, "Do you mind if I speak with Leah alone for a bit?" He answered, "Not at all," he gave me a kiss on the cheek and said, "I'll be outside." I looked at Leah and took a deep breath.

"Leah, can we please talk?" I desperately asked. "Sure," she replied, and we both sat down on the living room sofa. "I am so sorry," I said while looking directly at her. "I had no right to say what I said to you that day in the hospital." She didn't say anything right away but after a couple seconds, she said, "It's okay. That was a difficult day for both of us." She paused a moment then continued to say, "Julie, I want you to know that I never signed the divorce papers." "Oh," I responded. Then I noticed a tear running down her cheek as she said, "After his accident, I had a change of heart. I was going to tell him the day you and I had lunch but then...well, he was gone." I started to say, "I'm so sorry that- "but she quickly interrupted me. "Please, let me finish. "I loved your brother more than you could ever know, more than he knew but the divorce was my idea, he would have never left me." She sighed heavily. "I regret that decision now. I really thought Ben was going to survive and we would be here together today, living happily ever after." I gave her a smile and said, "I wish I could have been a part of you and Ben's life together."

Blake entered the room. "Everything okay in here?" he asked. Leah and I looked at each other and smiled. "Yes," I said, "everything is just fine." Leah and I got up from the sofa and as Blake and I were getting ready to leave, she asked, "Hey, why don't the two of stay here tonight instead of going back to the hotel?

We can eat a late dinner and drink some wine. I can tell you stories about Ben and share some memories with you." Blake and I briefly looked at each other but didn't answer her. "Um," she continued, "I think it would really be good for us, Julie." I agreed and Blake was fine with the idea, so we stayed. After a long night and one too many bottles of wine, morning came quickly, and Blake and I had to get up early to head back home.

During the drive, Blake surprised me by asking, "Do you want to postpone the wedding?" I replied, "No! Why would you ask me that?" He responded, "Well, you just lost your brother and so much has happened. I thought maybe you needed some time" I interrupted, "Blake I don't need time. I want to marry you. I can't wait to be your wife and for us to be a real family. It's what I need." He held my hand and said, "Ok then. We are getting married a week from Saturday." I smiled at him and said, "Yes, we are."

It was finally our big day! Both Amber and Leah were there but had not met each other before the wedding. I introduced them to one another, "Leah, this is Amber, Blake's sister and Amber, this is Ben's wife, Leah." As they were shaking hands, Amber said, looking at both of us, "I'm sorry for your loss. I can't imagine what the two of you must be going through right now." We both said thank you then I said, "Amber, why don't you sit with us for a while." Leah and I both moved over so Amber could sit next to us on the bench. I was in the middle. We were talking about Blake and Ben, sharing stories and memories. It was nice being able to laugh with each other. Then Dottie came over to us. "Well, you three ladies seem to be having a good time over here," she said. "Yes, Dottie," I replied, "we are." She then said, "It's been a wonderful wedding but it's almost over. You gals better get out on that dance floor before the band calls it quits." The three of us chuckled as Dottie walked away. I stood up and looked at Amber and Leah. "I just want both of you to know..." I was getting a little choked up, "the two of you have been here for me in ways neither of you could ever imagine." I turned to Amber and took her hand. "Amber, you have been like a sister to me, and I love you and your brother so much." Then I turned to Leah and took her hand, "and Leah," I said, as my eyes were welling up, "I am so thankful to have met you. Because of you, I was able to know who my brother was. I miss him so much and I know you do, too." I then smiled at each of them while sobbing and said, "I couldn't have asked for two better sisters-in-law." I wiped my tears as they both wiped theirs. They stood up and we hugged one another then I grabbed each of their hands and said, "Come on girls. We have some dancing to do."

And just like that, five years went by. Mia and Mandy were both away at college about three hours from home. Mia is studying to be a veterinarian and Mandy, a nurse. Timmy, well, Tim, as he now prefers to be called, attends a private school just a few towns over. I see the girls but not nearly as often as I'd like. They share a dorm room, so I feel comfortable that they are away together.

Three years ago, Dottie passed away from a brief battle with cancer. It was a tremendous loss for all of us. She was buried in a small private family cemetery in the woods behind her property, a part of the land I had not known existed, alongside Blake's mother and his wife and son. Blake had never told me about the cemetery or that his wife and son were buried there but I certainly didn't make a big deal out of it. I hoped that Blake would still visit their graves when he needed to. After all, they were a part of his life, long before I was. Dottie left her house to Amber and the Diner to me and Blake. I hired Amber as my manager and Tim works there on the weekends. Mandy will work a couple shifts here and there when she is home from college but Mia, well, she is always busy with her boyfriend Alex when she's not at school. Leah is always there to pitch in when I need her. Blake had a hard time when Dottie died, and Amber did as well. It was rough on each of us and Linda, too, as she and Dottie became close friends over the years.

Blake and I have been pretty busy once again remodeling the cabin. He added a sunroom in the back where we love to sit and watch the wildlife around us. Our relationship has grown so strong over the years. I still, to this day, cannot believe how lucky I was to meet him. Blake adopted the girls, and they now call him Dad. Soon after, we adopted a dog, a five-year-old Labrador Retriever named Paxton.

Before the girls left for college, I told them everything about their "real" father...and their grandmother, Linda. I didn't tell them what happened to Derek or Nancy, and I never will. They continue to have a good relationship with their grandmother, whom they now call Nana.

I have made many friends since acquiring the diner. Some I met through Dottie and some new ones. Blake has had a few of the guys over for barbecues that he knows from the tavern. All and all, we have a good group of friends we socialize with, and the three kids have several friends as well. Life truly could not be any better for us, but suddenly, everything would change.

It was a beautiful service. We were surrounded by family and friends. For the next several weeks, everyone was so kind and thoughtful, bringing us pre-cooked meals and casseroles, sending us cards and flowers, and offering to do whatever we needed done. We are still all in disbelief about what happened. My world, our world, was turned upside down within minutes, and I still didn't know how to cope. I didn't know how to make myself feel better let alone try to make everyone else. I visit the graves constantly and place flowers on each one. I sit for awhile and talk with them. It helps a little bit.

Then, one day, as I was walking back to the house, I saw Amber and Leah walking towards me. We met each other at the bench in the yard. We sat down, I was in the middle. Neither of us said anything right away then I looked at each of them and said, "The last time the three of us sat on this bench together was on my wedding day." They both sighed. I continued to say, "I can't believe they're gone. I wish I could have done something differently." I began to cry, and Leah held me and said, "There was nothing you could have done, nothing any of us could have done. It was a tragic accident," she took my hand and continued, "I miss them, too." She then looked at Amber and I, "and I can't imagine what you both are going through." There was silence then Leah said, "The three of us have certainly lost a lot in our lives. You and I, Julie, lost Ben and now, you and Amber have lost Tim and Blake. We will get through this, we will, together."

I have never been the same since losing Tim and Blake. The girls have had a difficult time as well, adjusting to life without their brother and father. I continue to ask myself and God, why this happened to us and question the events from that day. Why didn't I pick up Tim from school that afternoon? Was there a deer in the road? Were they joking and laughing as they so often did together right before the crash? Those questions and so many more kept going through my head.

We never knew the exact cause of the accident. We just knew Blake's truck slammed into a large boulder on the side of the road. I had just lost my adorable son and the love of my life. I can't fathom how I am supposed to go on without them, but I still have my daughters and they need me, now more than ever. We started out with just the three of us and now here we were, just the three of us, again. If there is any comfort to hold onto from any of this, it's knowing that neither of them died alone and Blake didn't have to go through the pain of losing another son.

After a while, I decided to go back to the diner and pick up where I had left off before the accident. Some commended me for moving on so quickly while others judged me for doing so. None of them had been through what I had been through, so it didn't matter to me what anyone thought. We were all trying to live life the best way we could while honoring Blake and Tim's memory.

Two years had passed and rather quickly I might add. Mia was attending graduate school six hours away and Mandy was a nurse, working at the same hospital where Tim was born. She was living in an apartment outside of town with her boyfriend. I would meet her for coffee in the hospital cafeteria often and I felt close to Tim when I was there.

The girls were doing okay, and I was so happy about that and proud of each of them. I, on the other hand, kept a lot of my feelings bottled up inside. I would still cry myself to sleep every night while holding Paxton tightly. Tim adored that dog and Blake was pretty fond of him, too. I had never really been a dog person, but I now felt connected to him because I knew he was hurting, too. Leah had moved away. She had an opportunity to work for a prestigious company in New York, so she took it. I miss her. Amber is still living in the house and has taken in a tenant for the cottage. She works full-time at the diner, still as my manager and I don't know what I *would do without her. She's my best friend and we visit the cemetery together every weekend. Sometimes, we bring a bottle of wine and just sit on the grass and reminisce. I think it really helps both of us.*

After all this time, we are still finding things out about one another that we've never known, and we have grown extremely close over the past years. So much so, she and I developed a "relationship." Not once had I ever thought I could or would fall in love with a woman, but I did. I was surprised when Amber told me she had been involved with a girl back in high school. It only lasted about a year, but she said she had always been attracted to women and she confessed to me that she was attracted to me since she first saw me. I was reluctant to tell the girls about Amber and me, but I didn't want to keep this secret from them for long so I, well, we, ended up telling both of them together when they were home for Christmas. It went much better than I would have expected. Both Mia and Mandy were happy for Amber and me. They understood what brought us together and supported us as a couple now. Amber could make even my darkest days a little brighter and because of her and my girls, I was able to go on. As for the Diner, well, some staff and customers accepted us for who we were now, and others did not. It really didn't bother either of us. We were happy and that was all that mattered.

One day, I came home from work and noticed Paxton lying on the kitchen floor, whimpering. I immediately called Mia and she told me to take him to a vet right away, so I did.

After about an hour of examination and numerous tests, the results came back. Paxton had an aggressive type of cancer and there was nothing they could do for him. I was devastated but I did not want him to suffer in pain, so I made the quick decision to put him down. Another loss, another heartache. In a way, it felt like I was losing Blake and Tim all over again. Paxton was buried next to them.

Ten years later Amber and I are still together but neither of us felt the need to marry. Mia is a veterinarian, married and has a beautiful girl named Hope and Mandy is a Nurse Practitioner. She is also married and has two twin boys, Michael, and Mathew. They are adorable. My sons-in-law are both wonderful men and amazing husbands to my girls. Though I don't get to see my grandchildren often, we always spend the holidays together.

I sold the cabin and moved into the house with Amber. It was a tough decision, but I felt better knowing I was just a short walk away from the cemetery which Amber and I still visit every weekend together. I have suffered enormous loss in my life, but I have been able to find happiness, too. My life has changed in so many ways, but I have adapted to those changes.

Since the day Jonathan died to the day Paxton died, and everything in between, the good and the bad, I have learned to embrace all the love I have ever been given and gave in return. I can't go back; I can only move forward. I'm getting older now and I don't know how many more years I have before I am again with those who I have lost but I'm going to enjoy the rest of my life. I have changed who I once was, and it has been a difficult road to get to where I am now. Not a day goes by I don't think of Timmy, Blake, and Ben, and I still think about Jonathan. I miss them all so much...but I do not miss Sara.

THE END

ABOUT THE AUTHOR

Jeanna M. Marescalchi is currently living in the city of Port Charlotte, Florida with her husband, Keith. They have been married for over thirty years. Her daughter, Shannon, and daughter-in-law, Francesca, live in the state of New Hampshire along with her one-year-old granddaughter, Joella. Her son, Chad, is a college student attending school in Maine. This is Jeanna's fifth self-published book, and she is always thinking about her next one. She enjoys writing pieces others can relate to and stories that entertain her readers. Filled with drama, mystery, romance, and thrills, you will surely want to keep reading her stories until the very end.

"Don't let anyone tell you that you can't accomplish something. Give it your all and if you should fail the first time, pick yourself up and try again!"

www.ingramcontent.com/pod-product-compliance
Lightning Source LLC
Chambersburg PA
CBHW072016150726
47999CB00002B/680